THE NAMELESS

THE NAMELESS

Liza Burgess

author HOUSE®

AuthorHouse™
1663 Liberty Drive
Bloomington, IN 47403
www.authorhouse.com
Phone: 1-800-839-8640

This novel is entirely a work of fiction. The characters and incidents portrayed are the work of the author's imagination. Any resemblance to actual persons, living or dead, events, or localities is entirely coincidental.

Published by AuthorHouse   04/12/2012

ISBN: 978-1-4678-9739-6 (sc)
ISBN: 978-1-4678-9740-2 (e)

Any people depicted in stock imagery provided by Thinkstock are models, and such images are being used for illustrative purposes only.
Certain stock imagery © Thinkstock.

This book is printed on acid-free paper.

Because of the dynamic nature of the Internet, any web addresses or links contained in this book may have changed since publication and may no longer be valid. The views expressed in this work are solely those of the author and do not necessarily reflect the views of the publisher, and the publisher hereby disclaims any responsibility for them.

CONTENTS

Part III

This novel is dedicated to my late Mother and my dear husband.

Two special people who always believed that one day, *I would put pen to paper.*

My acknowledgements to the Author House team for their close collaboration.

Sincere thanks to my family and friends who, after reading the early chapters of this novel, encouraged me to continue writing. A special thanks to Peter and Stacey who ensured that I completed this book. I also would like to thank Andy Dalton who designed the cover of my book.

"Love and hatred are not blind, but are blinded by the fire they themselves carry with them."

Friedrich Nietzsche, German philosopher (1844-1900)

"Fragrant oils bring joy to the heart."
Proverbs 27

PROLOGUE: 2011

The airport was fairly quiet that morning. This was partly due to the time of year. The February holidays were over and the schools had now reconvened, and Easter was yet to come. Hence the airport had only the usual bustle of businessmen flying to appointments, singles flying out for some sunshine for a few days, and airport staff going about their everyday business.

On the newspaper stands, the headlines were full of concerns about the uprising in North Africa, the probability of yet another airline strike, and a fall in world financial markets, all rather depressing reading.

The clock in the airport departure hall showed 10.28 and a voice over the tannoy could be heard inviting the remaining passengers for flight number 321 to go immediately to gate 57, as the plane was ready for departure.

It was around this moment that a young woman carrying a baby headed towards the restrooms. She was dressed simply in a long floral dress, a light coat, and a headscarf which covered her head and most of her face. As she walked into the toilets, she carefully looked around to ensure that there were no other people present. She then put her hand into her shoulder bag and took out a lighter. This was now her moment, she thought, a moment she had been planning for almost two months. Her mind went back an hour previously when she had washed the baby before taking her own shower. When they were both dry, she had massaged oils over both their bodies. Although not unpleasant, she could still remember the overpowering scent, the smell of which still clung to her. She knew this would assist her in the task she was about to undertake.

She shivered slightly, and a tear ran down her eye as she looked at the baby girl lying peacefully on the nappy rack. For one moment, she almost lifted her up and ran out, but her wish for revenge was stronger than anything else, and so she knew she would carry out what she had come to do.

She kissed the baby before taking the lighter and setting her alight. Her heart ached as she heard the baby scream, but there was to be no going back. This was her final chance; he had to pay the highest price possible, and this was it. She then set alight her own dress before lifting up the burning child, and with the strength she had left and as the heat engulfed her entire body, she stumbled out into the departure lounge.

A bystander, who thought she had heard screaming coming from the restroom, could only scream as what looked like a living torchlight fell to the ground. Two policemen standing further up the departure area began to run the few hundred metres. They too had smelt something burning but when they reached the bodies, there was little left that could be done. A sudden silence took over, and then people started screaming as they watched in horror, powerless to assist the mother or the child unified as one in what appeared to be a horrific death. As help arrived, passengers watched in vain as time took over and they lay together, dying; the sirens and paramedics could be heard making their way towards them.

They were a burning furnace, and the baby now lay still at her side, her little face burned beyond all recognition.

The mother died in the ambulance, and the only words that anyone listening would have heard were, "Oh my God!"

Over the following weeks, many people were to pronounce these words, and for many different reasons.

Part I

FIVE YEARS EARLIER

THE RECEPTIONIST

She had not been expecting a call from the agency that afternoon in early March. It had been a long, cold winter, and as she sat cuddled in front of a log fire in her lounge, reading the latest Sophie Hannah novel and sipping a mug of hot chocolate, she stopped for a moment to press on a CD.

It was one of her favourites, Ornella Vanoni, singing "Senza Te," music she had learned to love when dating her husband. *Oh my God*, she thought, smiling to herself. That was certainly not yesterday. They had met in the local supermarket when she had been hesitating as to which type of pasta to buy.

"Why don't you try this one?" she had heard a voice say. She had taken his advice, they had started chatting, and he invited her for a coffee, where they had discussed their favourite Italian dishes and had fallen in love.

They had married a year later, and she had never regretted her choice of husband. He was handsome, sure, but his gentle manner and his ability of always seeing the other side of the coin had soon made her realise that sometimes she could be too impulsive and certainly not as apt as he was at thinking things through right to the end. His job as an airline pilot meant he travelled extensively, and she often thought just how much responsibility he had to cope with. She was sure that she could never hold a job like that, always having to put the passengers first and finally getting very little praise for it. She knew that he was highly popular among the airline staff, but this did not bother her. She knew how much he loved her, and he had never given her any reason to doubt this fact. She loved him deeply, perhaps in a different manner, but she could not imagine life without him at her side.

The Italian CD continued, and it was now Patti Bravo singing, another favourite. Her husband had found her this compilation and she never tired of playing it, especially on a chilly afternoon like this one.

She thought of her son, who was presently studying history of art in a European university.

When he left the family nest at the tender age of seventeen, she had cried for a week. She missed him more than she could ever have imagined possible. She, who had always been nagging at him, either to tidy his room, complete his homework, or turn down the music which often blasted through the house. When he had passed his final examinations and informed them that he planned to apply to study six hundred miles away, she could not believe what she was hearing. However, with quiet determination, he had gone about completing his application forms and had been accepted for the University of his choice.

He had left home the previous September and, to her surprise, had settled down quickly and was enjoying his course very much. Her husband had told her it would be good for him, make him stand on his own two feet, but to her it was the idea of losing him, fearing that he may fall into bad company, that he may even become a stranger to her. All those ideas had flashed through her mind, but with time she had been accustomed to his being away from home, and she looked forward to his frequent visits—in fact, on this day she thought happily about how he was coming home in ten days time.

The phone rang as she was lost in her nostalgic thoughts; she jumped up quickly to answer it. To her surprise, it was the employment agency, asking her if she could present herself the following morning at the offices of an investment company in the centre of the city.

She was not sure if she was really ready for this. She had put in her CV a few weeks ago, a day where she had been feeling low and thought that perhaps a little job would do her good, not to mention that some pocket money would come in handy, to add to her everlasting collection of gorgeous handbags she had acquired over the past years. A weakness, yes, but it was like her books and music collection: luxuries in life that would be very hard for her to part with, a fact that she was more than proud to admit.

She had stopped working as PA to the CEO of a private bank last year. Why she had decided to resign, she was unable to explain either to the bank or to her husband. It was just one of these things she did in life, often on the spur of the moment. Not perhaps one of her best characteristics, but what was done was done, and she rarely if ever regretted any of her decisions.

She wondered sometimes if she had just wished for some precious time to herself, to indulge in her hobby of writing poetry and devouring books.

Now listening to the young lady at the other end of the line, she wondered what had possessed her to leave her CV with that agency. She would now have to face some interview tomorrow. As she noted down the address of the company, she thought that perhaps she could make an excuse, such as having a dental appointment or, better still, visiting friends out of town. But she did not provide such an excuse and found herself agreeing to be there at the given time. *Nothing really to lose*, she told herself as she put down the phone and returned to the more interesting factor of reading her book and listening to Patti.

She suddenly looked at her watch and realised that it would soon be time for her husband's flight to land. Lately, he had been travelling extensively; his job as a long distance airline pilot took him all over the world. She closed her book just as her mobile rang. From the number, she knew that it was him and prayed silently that he had returned safely. She answered the phone and found that he had indeed landed and was on his way home.

She set about preparing the table for a light lunch. Scrambled eggs and smoked salmon and a bottle of Sancerre to accompany it. A fresh baguette and some brie, and that would be it.

As she watched from the window, he came out of the taxi and she saw how tired he looked. She rushed to the door to welcome him home and saw the fine lines around his eyes, showing the fatigue, but the warmth of his smile as always made her heart melt.

They drank their wine and he told her a little of his trip—never too much. He handed her a box.

"Just a little surprise from my trip," he said. She opened the box and saw a beautiful string of pearls complete with a jade clasp.

"I love them, but you do spoil me," she told him. She knew that he always brought her a little gift when he returned from one of his numerous trips, and he never ceased to amaze her with his choice of gifts. She hugged him as he went to sit down at the table.

Let's eat now," he said. "Sit down and give me an update on all your news."

She told him about the call from the agency and her appointment the following day.

"That's great," he told her. "A part-time job is just what you need."

She asked him if he had heard about the company in question; he shook his head and told her he had heard the name but knew nothing of their comings and goings. Happy with this, she put the matter out of her head. She had more important things to think about . . .

The next day was dry, and a ray of sunshine made an attempt to pierce between the heavy clouds of the wintry morning. Spring was still a few weeks off, she thought, pulling up the collar of her classic camel-coloured coat. She decided not to take the bus but called a taxi; to hell with the expense, at least she would arrive at the interview looking her best. One last look in the mirror before departing, just to check her lipstick was right and she was ready to go.

The taxi dropped her off at the given address at around 10.15. She hated being late for anything, but looking at her watch, she realised that she was a little too early. She noticed that there was a little cafe just around the corner from the company and popped in and ordered an espresso.

She lit up a cigarette; a habit she had been trying to give up for months, but the odd one would not do her any harm, she always told herself. An excuse perhaps, but every rule had its exception.

The warm coffee together with the nicotine warmed her, making her feel rather relaxed. Upon finishing both, she paid the young waitress, popped a mint in her mouth, and made her way into the company's building.

As she went up the three steps to a glass door, she saw a guard or a security officer obviously waiting for her to advance through the door. She went through, giving her name, and at that precise moment, a lady in her early fifties appeared, extending her hand and giving her a warm smile. She was well groomed and dressed entirely in green, a colour she obviously liked. Her suit was pale green completed with a white shirt, with some type of green glass baubles hanging around her neck. The woman called over the security guard and introduced the newcomer. The woman explained that he would be accompanying her to the seventh floor, where the interview would take place. Nothing more was said, and she guessed that PR was not their strong point.

The elevator was like ones she had seen in the large city malls or some of the more luxurious hotels. *Well,* she thought, *they may not say a lot, but who cares? Perhaps the offices will be as elegant as the lift.*

She noticed that the young man held a magnetic card in his right hand, and she quickly glanced around to see if there were any security cameras. There were none, at least none that she could see. They finally reached the desired floor and she was requested once more to follow him.

He knocked on a very large decorative wooden door, with the title "Chairman" written on a brass plate. She heard someone say, "Come in," and the guard opened the door. She hesitated on the threshold before daring to step inside the room. Her first reaction was that she was entering what she thought to be a large boardroom. The office was very large and obviously had been furnished to impress.

There were six large windows surrounding the beautifully decorated office, which held elegant and elaborate furniture. A quick glance showed a variety of silver-framed photos placed around the small, highly polished tables; on the walls, there were many paintings, mainly of Arabian horses and Moorish-style buildings.

The chairman had the time to study the lady, who seemed more interested in admiring his office than introducing herself. Not that this displeased him. He knew his office often impressed and was therefore not surprised at her reaction. If the truth be known, he was happy with it.

After a couple of seconds, she turned her head to greet him and extended her hand. To his surprise, he found himself looking into a pair of bright green eyes. She smiled at him, and he smiled back at her as they shook hands warmly. He asked her to take a seat opposite him and invited her to introduce herself.

She knew that he must have read her CV, as it was lying in front of him, but nevertheless she proceeded to provide him with the relevant details. During this time, he was appraising her every move: the wide innocent look, the habit she had of placing her right hand through her blonde hair. He noticed that she was dressed in a tailored black suit. She wore pearl earrings with a silver chain around her neck. He noticed also that she wore an emerald ring on her left hand, the colour of her eyes, he thought, together with a white gold diamond wedding ring.

He decided there and then that he was going to hire her. This was not in line with his character. He prided himself in hand-picking each member of staff but always made sure that he saw at least two or three candidates for each post before making his final decision.

If he thought that the young lady facing him was listening to him, he was very wrong. She was in fact studying him carefully. What she saw was an immaculately dressed man in his early forties with a burnished complexion and brown eyes with very long eyelashes. His suit was cut to perfection, and his blue shirt and expensive tie all went together with the look. He had eyes like amber, eyes she thought that could change, becoming cold and hard if necessary.

His voice was deep and pleasing to the ear as she heard him speak. She suddenly realised that she had not been listening to what he had been asking her, but thinking she had caught the last phrase, she answered hesitantly, praying that she had understood his question.

"How about next week?" she answered. "Or at your convenience?"

"Next week is fine," he replied. "Do you have any questions you wish to ask?"

She summoned up the courage to ask if there would be any training, what exactly the part-time hours would be, and what salary he had anticipated for the position.

"Shall I have to see someone in Human Resources?" she asked.

"No," he replied. "I decide."

These were words that would echo in her ears in the years to come.

"As for your contract," he added, "my lawyers will draw this up, including your salary and working conditions. This will be a part-time position to commence with, probably two and a half days per week, but eventually the job could become full time, requiring your presence at least four if not five days a week. How do you feel about this?"

"Oh, that would be fine," she said. She was happy to commence part-time with a rather generous salary, and the thought of eventually working full time did not bother her.

The chairman glanced at his watch, which she took to be a subtle hint that the interview had now ended.

Standing up, she thanked him for his time, and suddenly there was a knock at the office door. As if by magic, the young security guard appeared. He had arrived as if an invisible bell had rung to summon him, a bell only audible to his ears.

She went back down with him in the lift and was relieved that there was nobody around at the reception. She caught the bus home and was glad to hear the crying of children and the noise of the usual crowds on the public transport. She had never been so glad to hear such everyday noises, after the disturbing silence of the chairman's office.

Descending at her bus stop, she walked the five hundred metres home, kicked off her high heels, and put on the television. Making her way into the kitchen, she opened the fridge, chose a bottle of white wine, and poured herself a rather large glass.

What is wrong? she thought, sipping her wine and finding herself finally beginning to relax. *Something is not quite right here. Why would a chairman interview someone for a part-time job?* She had never seen or heard anything quite like it in her life.

Not to worry, she would tell her husband the whole episode over dinner. He would laugh and tell her that she was imagining things and worrying over nothing.

As she raised her glass to her lips, she smiled. Yes, everything was going to be just fine.

She would remember this moment several years later.

THE CHAIRMAN

The chairman looked at his watch and saw that it was already 16.45. He called his secretary and asked for a long distance call. *Better to get this business matter over with before leaving for home,* he thought.

After the call was done, he rang his chauffeur, who had been in his service for almost seven years, and asked him to have the Bentley ready in front of the office in around ten minutes. He normally liked to drive to the office, but recently, he had been using his chauffeur more and more. True, that was what he was paid to do, as he placed various documents in his leather briefcase.

With a press of a button, the security guard was there to accompany him to the car. It passed his mind sometimes that he would be just as comfortable without all these trappings of wealth, but then money had to be spent, and he felt that in this manner, he kept people employed. He sometimes wondered if this was just an excuse he gave himself.

His mind went back to his meeting with the young lady that morning. She had somehow managed to unsettle him. He did not like that, as he prided himself on perceiving people quickly. It was, after all, just a position for a receptionist, but she had been proud, intelligent, and not very submissive, he thought, something he was accustomed to in his position. He knew that she had been impressed with his office but was less sure that he had impressed her.

He knew that he had everything anyone could wish for in his life. A beautiful wife, two teenage children, and as much money as he could ever spend. So what was worrying him about hiring a new receptionist? He must be coming down with the flu, he thought to himself as the chauffeur arrived to collect him at the office door.

The Bentley was royal blue; all his cars were of the same colour. Blue was a colour he had always liked. He thought of his wife and her cornflower blue eyes and laughed. Yes, he did have everything he could wish for; he began to relax on the short journey home.

The chauffeur glanced in the mirror and noticed that the chairman looked a little tired and strained. Surely he must have some business matter on his mind. The chauffeur would have done anything for his boss. He had hired him a number of years back when he lost his job as a technician with Alfa Romeo. Ever since then, he and the boss had become friends, and there was nothing he would not have done for him. He was a real gentleman who knew how to treat his staff with the utmost respect, not a common trait among the elite. As they approached the villa, another security guard appeared instantly. Timing was a priority in this job, and the staff constantly kept in touch with each other whenever the boss was on the move. The iron gates opened with a flick of a remote control.

The chairman descended from the car without any other words other than "Thank you," and he walked towards his home. The chauffeur, knowing he was no longer required, signed the security log book, noting their time of arrival, and left it with the security guard. He then picked up his small Renault, a gift from the chairman last year, and set off home to his family. Another day without any major problems, he sighed with relief.

Meanwhile, the chairman proceeded to the entrance of his vast villa. It was obviously built to please the eye, the entrance having been designed to resemble a Japanese garden. There was also an outside cottage which was used solely for the domestic staff. There were tennis courts to the left of the house, and although not used often enough, they were a constant reminder of the fact that he could afford this, and more. As it was not yet spring, the floodlights lit up the entire garden, giving it an almost fairylike and ethereal look. It appeared to the onlooker as though the trees were dancing and the shadows of the bushes were part of the audience, clapping their hands in delight at their every move.

The flowers were not yet in bloom, but one could only imagine the splendour of the cherry trees in full bloom, come the month of April. The most beautiful rose garden led to the front door; during the summer months, it resembled an archway of cascading petals and sweet scent.

The garden, like many of his possessions, never gave him any real satisfaction. It was another object for him but he never took the time to admire the wonderful array of colour that would come with the forthcoming season. True, he hired two gardeners to look after the grounds, but he never experienced any of the real pleasure in tending personally over the numerous shrubs and flowers. He paid people to do such tasks, assuming that if someone was paid to work, then they should get on with the job in question. As far as domestic staff went, that was his steadfast rule.

As usual, no one came to the door to welcome him.

As was his custom, he took off his shoes in the glass porch prior to entering the house. He proceeded directly into the lounge, where the maid came rushing forward to ask if he required any refreshments. The lounge was like a picture out of *Country and Life*. It was a stunning eighty-square-metre room overlooking the water. There was a mezzanine raised above the lounge, and hanging above the huge Italian fireplace was the latest television and recording equipment anyone could imagine.

He asked the maid about his wife and children. She informed him that his wife was in town shopping, his daughter was attending her ballet classes, and his son was at his football training.

As always, they were all busy. He phoned his wife on her mobile. She was brief and told him that she would be home shortly. He did not worry about his son; he was like his father and could take care of himself, but his daughter of eighteen was another matter. He rang her mobile but to no avail. *Daughters are all the same*, he thought. *She has everything a young girl of that age could wish for.*

There were moments when even he knew that he spoiled her too much; in fact, his wife reminded him often of this fact. He thought about the custom-made gold bracelet he had ordered for her birthday next month. It was to be a surprise. He knew that she was hoping for a car, having recently passed her driving test, but he had decided for her own safety, to wait a little longer before presenting her with the convertible car he knew she wanted so badly

His daughter was a candle in his life, and he gave into almost all of her whims; moreover, he knew that she was well aware of this. She had begun talking about going to the States next year, either to study fashion or perhaps find work in a fashion magazine. Well, time would tell. He had an idea of ordering a Mini Cooper for her next year. This would surely keep her happily at home, without having to dash to the other side of the world. He had a slight suspicion that his wife may even be encouraging her to grasp her freedom and take flight in order to find her independence, but he would handle this matter with her later on. He knew how to get around his wife, or at least he used to. She had changed recently and had become a little distant with him, and so he had avoided bringing up the subject of their daughter's plans for the time being. However, he knew that they would soon have to discuss her future. She was, after all, their only daughter, despite the fact that he and his wife were from different nationalities and did not share the same religion.

Completely lost in his thoughts, he did not hear his wife come into the room. He turned around at the sound of a door opening. He still loved his wife after twenty-one years of marriage, and her smile and deep blue eyes never ceased to please him.

She was wearing a bright red dress which enhanced her ample cleavage, something he felt was unnecessary for an afternoon in town. He did not always approve of her dress choice, and recently her attitude was one of, how could he explain it, perhaps that of "Well, here I am so what's new?" He wondered if she really now cared what he thought. It had not always been this way, but things had changed over the past few years, or was it he who had changed? The thought perplexed him.

He knew that he could go anywhere and buy pleasure but this was not his principle; an odd fling, perhaps, but it was his wife he hungered after, and recently she was not too forthcoming. It had crossed his mind that she may have found someone else, but who and where? Where did she disappear to, in the afternoons? Not knowing made him angry, and yet he feared asking her. He wondered if he was becoming too possessive, not only with her but also with his children.

She had begun to be distant and slightly vague about her whereabouts, and he wondered deep down that she may be unhappy living here. She was originally from one of Europe's northern countries, and her stunning looks were a mixture of brunette hair and bright blue eyes, a turn-on for most men.

He had even thought of asking security to note down the exact time she left the villa and also when she returned, but decided to do nothing about this for the time being. Discretion was one of his main priorities, both in his personal life as in his professional one; therefore, such an idea appalled him. Yet at the same time, he had been tempted to carry it out.

The door opened yet again, and this time, it was his daughter, who flew into the room, arms outstretched, ready to give him a hug, something she knew he loved. She was very pretty to the eye, tall with long black hair, a trait she had inherited from her father. She was slim and dressed in the latest fashion. She wore a short pink dress with beige pumps, and to complete the outfit, a jacket in a pale shade of mauve. Daddy did spoil her, and she knew that if she was very clever, he would finally give in and agree to her moving to the States. She knew that her mother would help, but then again, Daddy was another matter. She would have to play her cards right the first time, for with him, there was no going back on matters. "I decide," he liked to reiterate, and decide he always did.

The family sat down in front of the fireplace, the logs burning brightly, making pretty shadows on the wall. The maid brought in a jug of fruit juice, and they sat in silence, waiting for someone to speak. Suddenly the final member of the family arrived into the comfort and warmth of the lounge, breaking into the loud silence. The latest arrival, their son, who was not yet seventeen, was fairly short in height, rather plump but with a mop of brown hair and a most attractive smile. "The little one," as they called him, was still wearing his football shorts and t-shirt, which his mother kindly asked him to remove and take down to the laundry room for the maid to wash the following day. She then added that he should shower and change before joining the family for dinner.

Several minutes later, the maid came in and announced that dinner was served. Tonight they were eating Asian, something the family loved; for the chairman, the spicier the food, the better it tasted.

Around the table, there was little conversation; there rarely was. This was mainly due to the fact that the chairman had taught his children that a dining table was a place to eat, not a place to chatter incessantly.

The meal finished, the family retired to the lounge. The children decided to retreat to their respective rooms, and for the first time that day, his wife asked the chairman how things were going. He mentioned that he planned to hire a new receptionist to work part-time along with the other girl, but he avoided giving out any details. He had recently made it a habit never to discuss business matters with his wife. It must be said that it had not always been this way. There had been a time when they would both sit up talking all night about their future aims, trying to put the world to right, but those days had long gone, particularly over the past seven years. He glanced over at her and thought how beautiful she still was, but she was already flicking through the *TV Guide* and barely listening to what he was saying to her.

His thoughts returned to business and the company he and his partner had set up several years ago. They had recently moved offices to a new location, and he was hoping that with a bit of luck, business would expand and the investment market would eventually start booming again. He knew for a fact that one of the hedge fund companies down the road was up for grabs; after much deliberation with his partner, they had decided to put in a bid. This would give them a wider scope and at the same time enable the company to expand further into new emerging markets, an area which he thought was the wisest place to invest, at least for the time being.

This acquisition would provide them with an additional five young investors, mainly all in their late thirties and early forties, and along with the two young investors he and his partner had brought in six months ago, the company should quickly bring in strong dividends.

It was essential to his lifestyle that he always had a large amount of liquidity. His wife and children required a lot of money to keep them in the style they had become accustomed to (or rather the lifestyle he had chosen to provide them with), not to mention the two houses he had to maintain. He had acquired a rather large prestigious chalet up in the mountains a couple of years back, only a three-hour drive from their main residence.

They had been on a skiing holiday when they had come across this beautiful "wooden house," as his son had called it, with its magnificent views down the valley and across the mountains. Stepping inside, any guest would have difficulty taking in at a glance the vast lounge with its huge bay windows, wooden beams, and enormous log fire. The room was furnished with warmth and hospitality in mind. Three large cream sofas with a chintz pattern were placed around the room; each sofa had a cashmere throw—over in one of the colours of the chintz. At each side of the sofas were wooden tables all adorned with the most amazing lamps, the base being of creamy white porcelain and the lamp shades, a rich warm wine colour. In front of the fireplace was placed a white wooden coffee table, complete with a glass top. Underneath this glass was the most fabulous collection of Faberge eggs, some in the deepest shades of blue and gold, others in a lighter tone of blue, and others the colour of yellow primroses, all encircled with the distinctive gold rim. The smallest ones were of various colours and could be opened to portray the jeweller's intricate artistic designs. No two eggs were alike. These eggs had been a gift to his wife over the years, on her birthday or their wedding anniversary, and she had lovingly brought them up to the chalet, where they had enchanted many of their neighbours.

The walls of the lounge were painted a stark white, and on these walls he had invested in many modern paintings, all of them with vibrant colourings. The splashes of red, yellow, blue, and green only lent additional warmth to this exceptional room. Looking upwards, visitors could admire the gallery, where there was a large wooden railing around half of the lounge; he was always tempted to look down from upstairs just to admire the setting.

Perhaps he should take his wife and children up to the mountains during the forthcoming spring break, he thought. It was time that they all got together as a real family, and with a bit of luck, he and his wife could sort out some of the differences and perhaps start off on a new footing. It may be difficult, he thought, but well worth the effort.

With that out of his mind, his thoughts moved on to the large business event he and his partner were planning shortly. Their idea was to invite la crème de la crème within the banking and industrial sector and outline their future investment plans. If the acquisition went through prior to this gathering, it would give the new company just the right exposure they needed. He had not spoken of this to anyone so far, but upon reflection he thought that the young lady he had hired that same morning would be just the perfect person to prepare such an event. Her CV had been excellent, and he knew perfectly well that she was overqualified for the position on offer. However, good personnel were a valuable asset to any company, and she could well turn out to be just that. He had taken an instant liking to her, and she had impressed him with her quiet dignity and charm.

He also thought that shortly he would have to start looking for a new chauffeur. His faithful friend was getting on, and at the age of sixty-six, he realised that it was time he retired, thus enabling him to return to the warmth of the South from where he originated. It would be hard to find someone so dedicated, but he had decided to take on a young man, who could not only act as his chauffeur when necessary but also carry out some odd jobs around the estate. If the truth be known, he did not really require a full-time chauffeur, and knowing that his wife would never wish to be driven anywhere, the idea pleased him. He would of course rely on his present chauffeur to assist him in selecting the right substitute. He could share his partner's chauffeur, but somehow this idea did not appeal to him. He preferred to find someone who would report only to him.

He began to feel weary and finally arose, announcing to his wife that he was turning in for the evening. He liked to retire early, contrary to his wife. He sometimes wondered why they still slept in the same bedroom, as she preferred to stay up half the night on that computer of hers, although what she did exactly, he had no idea. However, he had to admit that she was an excellent mother to their two children, and they both loved her dearly. She was never to be seen at the breakfast table, but she was always there for them, whatever their needs.

I must have changed, he thought. They used to have such fun when they were younger, living up North. He knew that he had become withdrawn and that he no longer was able to fill her life with the joy and laughter she so loved and longed for. He no longer drank alcohol and had asked her to do likewise. She had agreed, but since this arrangement, he felt he had lost her somehow. Nothing he could pinpoint, but he had noticed that she had begun to drift away from him, little by little, but at the same time, he had done nothing to rectify the matter. His daily prayers were of comfort to him, and he wondered if he did not find solace in this particular path. If only she had decided to share these beliefs with him. Seven years was a long time living in a strange city, and she had few friends, of that he was certain.

He prayed on his knees, as had become his habit, before falling asleep with only the sound of his watch, ticking regularly and breaking through the dark evening silence.

Tomorrow he was flying off to a business meeting for a few days. Perhaps things would be better upon his return, was his last thought, as sleep overtook his mind and body.

THE LOBBYIST

He had been born wealthy, with a silver spoon in his mouth, his friends liked to remind him. Indeed he had and knew this better than anyone. However, strangely enough, it had never bothered him. He liked money and had the bad habit of taking his wealth for granted.

He had been an only child, a delightful surprise for his parents, who had long given up hope of ever having children. Hence, he lacked for nothing, and his mother in particular made sure of this. He attended the best private schools and completed his studies at Harvard, graduating with honours in law and economics at the age of twenty-four.

Law somehow had attracted him, and with his father's help, he soon found himself set up in his own business in the best district of the city. He had no interest in helping others less fortunate than he, neither did he see himself pleading in the courtroom for some poor sod who had premeditated a murder and who eventually might seek him as his defence lawyer. He had other ambitions, and this he was certain he could obtain through corporate law.

Business went well over the following years, and he soon found himself being invited to all the swanky functions and mixing with the elite of the town. His father (a well-known and highly respected senator) had been a great assistance to him in the first few years which had gone a long way in his quick ascension. However, he now felt that his success was basically down to his own hard work and efforts. He had good looks, a quick wit, and a profound love of the good life; his mother often asked if he had any intention of settling down one day. He knew that what she was actually asking was when he planned to marry.

Marriage, to her, meant settling down with a young wealthy heiress and having children and a dog.

This was not in the cards right now. He often met the type of young lady who would appeal to his mother, the ones who worked on charitable committees and wore the standard uniform of Chanel suits complete with two strings of pearls, not forgetting the impeccable make-up and the ever present smile. He avoided these women like the plague, although he had to admit that on several occasions, he had enjoyed a fling with a few of them and had found, to his great surprise and pleasure, that without the suit and pearls, they could be a bit on the wild side. But after a while, they bored him, and he reverted to the life he had chosen, that of the golf course, a woman whenever he felt the need, and the freedom that goes with such a life.

His status led to a 200-square-metre penthouse overlooking the park. His was a duplex with a beamed loft, where he kept all his precious mementos, such as his first edition books and endless collection of jazz and classical music. It was here that he enjoyed relaxing when he was at home. His den, he called it and planned to keep it that way. All this belonged to him, and for the time being he had no intention of sharing it with anyone or inviting intruders into his world. The rest of his home was situated on the lower floor.

The kitchen was state-of-the-art in gleaming chrome, with black and silver furniture. Here, he often enjoyed entertaining friends or business colleagues, and his speciality was preparing them his vodka shake, a mixture of vodka, hot sauce, and a touch of lime. He knew he drank more than he should, but life was there for the taking, and he was not ready in any way to give up this lifestyle.

However, a chance meeting in a local restaurant would change all that. He had been kept late at the office with a client who had a serious litigation case, and even he had not found the courage to bring the meeting to an early closure. So it was that he found himself walking home around eight o'clock and passed in front of one of the French bistros recently opened in his area. He decided that he could not be bothered cooking anything that evening and decided to give the bistro a try.

Upon entering, he asked for a small table and found himself sitting near an attractive young lady in her midthirties. She was sipping a glass of white wine, and he assumed that she was not expecting company, as the table was set for one. Her face was vaguely familiar but from where, he could not fathom out.

He arose from his table and walked to the bar, where he ordered double vodka on ice. There was music playing softly in the background, and he thought it was a new version of Edith Piaf's famous hit from 1960, "Mon Dieu." He asked the barman if his guess was correct and this was instantly confirmed.

Quite chuffed with himself, he picked up his glass and made his way back to his table; on the way, he stopped and smiled at the young lady. She smiled back, showing off a perfect set of white, even teeth. She had a pleasant smile which warmed her eyes.

"Are you enjoying the music?" he said on the spur of the moment.

"Yes, it's rather nice," she answered.

"Are you dining alone?" he asked, more of an afterthought than anything else.

"Yes," she replied naturally. "I am just relaxing after a long hard day at the Senate." It clicked then where he had seen her.

"Mind if I join you?"

"Why not?" she replied. "I have not as yet ordered."

"Well, that makes two us, so let's order now," he added, introducing himself.

They finished their drinks, and he beckoned to the waiter, who appeared immediately.

"*Bonsoir Monsieur, désirez-vous voir la carte?*"

Before he had time to reply coherently, the woman said, "*Oui, mais qu'est ce que vous avez à nous proposer ce soir?*"

"*Le coq au vin est excellent, Madame.*"

"*Très bien, alors deux fois et puis nous aimerions voir la carte des vins.*"

He sat listening. So, she was intelligent as well as attractive, he thought. His school French had deserted him, and he was more than happy to let her take charge.

The sommelier brought the wine list over to their table, and after glancing through it, and without wishing to look overconfident, he chose a Bordeaux Lafitte 1989. *To hell with the expense*, he thought.

"A wonderful choice," his lady companion remarked casually.

"So tell me, where did you learn to speak such good French?"

"I speak only a little, but it's adequate," she replied modestly. "My grandmother was French, and I learned what I know from her and of course my own mother."

Their meal arrived; the wine was tasted, and they both agreed it was excellent, as they continued the evening with light conversation. As he paid the bill, he could not remember the last time he had enjoyed himself so much. She had a natural charm and was certainly delightful company.

They finished their meal and, after coffee, decided to call it a night. He told her that he was leaving for a few days on business, but that he would give her a call upon his return. They left the restaurant; he hailed her a taxi and proceeded to walk the short distance home.

He thought of their evening as he poured himself a nightcap and was surprised that she was still on his mind. He packed a few things in a weekend bag in preparation for his flight the following day, putting some papers together in his leather briefcase. Then he went to bed.

His car was waiting for him at eight o'clock in the morning to take him to the airport. As he checked in, he was glad that his seat number, 1C, was reserved for him. His secretary knew that he liked to fly first class whenever possible, a treat that he offered himself when flying more than three hours.

He was not one of those travellers who enjoyed passing the time chatting incessantly to his fellow travellers, not to mention screaming kids running up and down the aisle. No, first class was expensive but well worth paying the price for some peacefulness. The air hostess accompanied him to his seat, front row, window seat; perfect, he thought, thinking already of the first drink he would shortly be offered. That particular morning, however, he learned that he was going to have a companion on the aisle seat next to him.

Damn, he thought. He had seen the gentleman in question boarding. A man in his early forties, he thought, but his nationality was rather more difficult to guess. He was tall with black hair slightly receding from his forehead. He had a bronzed complexion but the colour was not from a suntan. He was dressed entirely in black: black trousers, black shirt, black brogues, and a prominent black belt with a silver buckle around his waist, the image he could not quite make out. *Who the hell is this?* he said to himself. *Looks like some ageing rock star or an actor from a television series years back.*

The man sat down. No words passed between them until three hours into the trip. He had noticed that his "companion," for use of a better word, drank only mineral water as he ordered his third vodka.

It was then that the man at his side spoke.

"Are you travelling on business?" he asked.

He replied that indeed he was but gave no further information. The man, however, continued, "What exactly is your line of business?"

He did not know whether to answer this question or not. But the vodka had relaxed him, so he replied that he was a lawyer and did the occasion lobbying whenever requested. *That should keep him quiet*, he thought with a smirk.

The man nodded but made no other attempt to converse. The lobbyist lifted his glass and soon realised that his companion was now snoozing, or did he imagine that his lips were moving. Could he be praying? *Oh my God*, he thought, *maybe I should slow down on the drink!*

The journey continued smoothly, and it was not too long before he heard the hostess announce that they would shortly be approaching their destination, requesting all passengers to ensure that their safety belts were securely fastened.

It was then that his companion spoke once again.

"How long do you plan to be in town?" he asked. His travelling companion then handed him a business card and added, "We have things to discuss; give me a call when you have time."

The lobbyist was slightly taken aback. People often remarked that he could be abrupt and to the point, but this man beat the record. He glanced at the card he had been given and handed over one of his own to the man, who said only seven words: "Fine, I shall be expecting your call."

The plane touched down, and the man disappeared out of the plane immediately, with only a small briefcase in hand. The lobbyist looked once again at the card he had been given. He was chairman of an investment company, one he knew nothing about. However, as he collected his luggage at the carousel, he knew that he would contact him. His curiosity had gotten the better of him, and he now wanted to know who the hell he was dealing with and, more importantly, why.

It would not be long before he found out.

THE CHAIRMAN'S WIFE

S he was beautiful, of that there was no doubt. She had been told often enough. However, as she awoke that morning and looked in the mirror, she felt far from being anything other than very tired.

She looked at the clock on her bedside table which showed 11.30. Not surprising, she thought, as it had been well past three o'clock before she had finally gone to bed. Her husband had been sleeping for hours, and she knew that he would be getting up around five o'clock to pray. That was now his routine and had been for the past few years. After that, she knew he spent some time down in the gym on his exercising machines, before showering and dressing for the day. He was very particular about his dress code and changed his suits most days. His shirts were starched in town, and his ties were always of the best design. He always had breakfast with the children, before seeing them off to school, driven by the security guard. He then left for town and to the office. Sometimes he drove himself, but recently he had been using his chauffeur a great deal. She sometimes thought it would be amusing to meet him in the hallway as she was going to bed and he arising for the day, but so far they had managed to avoid this scenario.

She had become used to this way of life; although for her it was a lonely existence. She had few friends, and her husband had changed so much over the past years. He was such fun when she had met him over twenty years earlier. She was not entirely sure if she could put this down to his religion, although she knew it played a large part in his "new" style of life. If only things could be as they had been many years ago, she sighed inwardly.

She threw on her dressing gown, a navy and mauve silk kimono with pale pink butterflies, and made her way downstairs. As always, the maid had prepared her a tray with freshly pressed orange juice, croissants, and marmalade, complete with compote de fruit. To finish off the tray, there was the delicious aroma of freshly ground coffee.

As she poured out her coffee, her mind went back many years; things had been so different then.

She had all the trappings of wealth and yet she knew that she was desperately unhappy. She loved her children and, at times, her husband, but there was something so different about him that she no longer truly felt part of his life. Taking the tray into the lounge, she sat down on the large sofa, placing the tray in front of her on the large coffee table. Her mind wandered back, and she thought of Mama, who repeatedly warned her about marrying so quickly, especially to someone of a different culture and faith. "You know so little about him," her mother had told her many times. And yet, she had gone ahead and married him. Now thinking back, perhaps Mama had been right all along, but they had been so much in love at the time. Nobody could have penetrated the fortress they had built around themselves. She sat quietly, reflecting on this, and began to remember how they had first met.

She had been born in the very north of Europe and had never known her father, something which had never troubled her. Her mother had covered all her needs, even when she was growing up into an adolescent. Mama was her best friend, and she had always known that no matter what happened in life, she would be there for her. Little did she know at the tender age of seventeen how true this would be, in the years to come?

She had always been popular at school and had been voted head pupil for the year, more than once.

She was also intelligent, and the fact that she was bilingual became a strong asset. Her mother had been born in Hungary and had always insisted that they spoke her native language in the long winter evenings, when they sat around the fire chatting as they placed more logs on to the blazing fire. The room where they sat most evenings was always warm, and the glow from the chimney, never ceased to provide additional warmth to their already cosy surroundings.

She passed her final exams at school with top marks and was awarded a scholarship at one of the city's finest universities. She thought about being an engineer, but at the same time, she loved architecture. She finally chose the latter.

Her first year went well, and she coped adequately with her course and the occasional odd jobs she managed to procure, jobs that she could handle with her university schedule. Her mother was a seamstress by trade and kept her in the latest fashion and colours, much to the envy of her fellow students. Jeans was the standard dress code, but she always had that extra touch, something special that Mama had dreamed up for her.

She was in her third year, progressing well, when she read in the local paper that a private jet company was looking for a part-time air hostess. *Well, why not give it a try?* she thought laughingly.

She knew that she had no experience whatsoever in this field, but if she could grasp a part-time job now, when she had fewer courses and less classes throughout the week, this would bring in some extra money, and Mama could work a little less.

And so it was, that after sending away her application complete with CV (not forgetting to attached a recent photo of herself; this was obligatory), she received an answer from the company a week later. In it, they asked her to present herself at the airport the following Wednesday, providing her with the time and the name of the person she would be seeing.

She had decided not to mention this matter at home. There were several reasons for this, but mainly she did not wish her mother to think that she was giving up her studies after so much hard work. *After all, nothing may come out of this*, she told herself. *I have only been asked to attend for an interview, as will many others, so why worry Mama unnecessarily?*

The following week passed quickly, and soon the day dawned for her interview. She hesitated before dressing that morning. Normally, she wore casual clothes to university but wanted to look her best that day. She finally decided on a royal blue suit. It had a short skirt which showed off her toned legs to perfection. The jacket was simple with a Peter Pan collar and a small pleat down the back. Around her waist, she wore thin red leather belt. She also wore a pair of high-heeled navy shoes and threw a large red leather handbag over her shoulder. Her only jewellery was a pair of pearl earrings which had been a gift from her mother the previous Christmas.

Looking in the mirror, she checked her hair was in place, the fringe not too much over her eyes, and added a touch of her favourite lipstick, burnt orange. *There*, she thought, *I am ready and really do not look too bad!* What she did not add was the fact that her suit matched her bright blue eyes; her eyelashes were so long and dark that neither mascara nor eye shadow was necessary to enhance them.

Her mother was busy working in her "workshop," as she liked to call it, cutting a pattern for a future bride. Her mother was too busy concentrating to see her leave the house, thus avoiding any questions as to where she was going. She did not relish the thought of having to make up some story or other.

She caught the bus to the airport, a trip which lasted around forty minutes. Upon arriving at the main terminal, she asked at the information desk where the offices were located. She was quickly directed to take the lift to the third floor and she would find the company, second office on the right.

She took a deep breath before knocking and walking in. The offices were not large but were set out in an open space manner, where she could see desks piled high with dossiers. There were a couple of young girls sitting at two other desks, typing very fast.

Nobody gave her a glance, and she was about to leave, thinking that perhaps she had come to the wrong office, when a man suddenly asked, "Have you come for the hostess job? You must be the 11.30 appointment."

She was so grateful that someone had actually acknowledged her presence that she turned round and smiled before answering, "Yes, that is correct."

What a picture, the guy thought as he caught her lovely face for the first time. *Those eyes, oh my God, she could be a model*, he thought to himself. She was just what the company was looking for, and her CV was certainly an impressive one.

They sat down and she explained a little about herself, the importance of her studies and the fact that she could only work certain days per month. He explained what the job entailed, assuring her that she would only be on call a few days per month. She would often be told two days prior to flying that she was needed, but he could not promise this would always be the case. She nodded in agreement, listening attentively, although from time to time, her mind wandered to the courses she might miss.

He stressed that this was a job that would not take her away from her studies, but that she had to be prepared for a little flexibility. The salary was good, and as he continued, she learned that the company was not an airline, but more like a society which let out private jets, either to wealthy individuals or industries whose top management often wished to use a private jet for particular meetings. He went on to identify the various type of aircrafts they used, such as Learjets and Falcons for short journeys, but also in the larger range, G 5s and Challengers. They had recently acquired a Gulfstream and were shortly expecting a delivery of a Global Express, the top range of the market, he explained.

These names were not familiar to her, and she began to feel a little naive at not knowing any of them.

He continued to fill her in regarding the training she would require. She had to learn the safety regulations and also would have to complete a Red Cross Training exam. Upon successfully completing these exams, she could well be considered for the job.

Finally, he asked her if she had any questions; in the event that she got the position, he asked her when she could anticipate commencing. She replied that she could start in six weeks time, giving her ample opportunity to finish her third year and also to complete the training course he had mentioned.

"Fine," he replied, "we shall be in touch shortly."

A letter arrived a week later, informing her she had successfully passed the interview and requesting that she commence her safety regulation course and the essential Red Cross training. Several dates were provided.

The last paragraph also outlined that upon successful completion of these courses, she would be offered the job and should be prepared to commence on July 1.

She cried out and wept with joy, running downstairs to announce the news to Mama.

Mama had not been over the moon about the matter, even after she explained exactly what her job would entail.

"What is all this nonsense about flying around the country, and not even in a real plane?" she had argued. "What on earth made you do such a thing, you who are normally so sensible?"

She sometimes regretted having told her mother that it was not a commercial airline, but she had thought that the idea of a small private jet would excite her. This had not been the case. Mama was far more concerned that she passed her third year exams than having her daughter flying around the world as an air hostess.

"You did not do all these years of studying to end up like a waitress," she had told her daughter one evening. These remarks had hurt, and so she decided to leave things alone and not bring up the subject again, at least not for the time being.

Her finals at university went well, even the oral, which she was never too keen about. To her, this part of the exam always depended on pulling the right straw, getting the right examiner facing you in order to make sure that anything you said could be justified and clarified in the correct and precise manner. She was pretty sure that she had passed her university exams but would have several weeks before this fact was acknowledged.

Now, with exams over, she could take her training courses, hopefully pass them, and start her new job.

Life continued as usual, but a little bit of her and Mama's intimacy was gone, or was it the fact that she was growing up and becoming her own person? Perhaps Mama resented this fact somewhere in her heart.

She passed her training courses with flying colours and soon July 1 arrived, the sun glowing in the bright blue sky. She had been awake since four o'clock that morning, partly due to excitement and partly due to the sun rising so early in that part of Europe. She dressed carefully, kissed Mama goodbye and told her that she would be back home later that evening for dinner.

The company had told her that she would be provided with a uniform; the first day would be spent taking her measurements for any necessary alterations, reading up the company's rules and regulations, and also spending some time with their human resources department. She had also been told that it would possibly be another eight days before she would undertake her first flight.

The first week passed quickly, and soon she was called in to the offices to be given her first flying destination and also given the instructions that had been provided by the company hiring the jet. She learned that this was standard procedure; each company had different demands and requests which they provided when chartering a plane.

Finally, the day dawned when she would be flying for the first time on a private jet. The plane would be a Gulfstream 150, taking five passengers on a two-hour flight.

She dressed like a bride for her nuptials that morning. The uniform was bright red suit with a white cotton shirt. She had the choice of several neckties, and for that first morning, she chose to wear a striped one. She tied the scarf in what she thought looked like *the Hermes look*, added a string of pearls, the only jewellery that was permitted, other than her small pearl earrings and a watch.

She was wearing the standard sheer tights complete with navy shoes with a moderate heel. She had pulled back her hair into a chignon and made up her face, using the minimum of make-up. She went downstairs, where Mama had prepared her breakfast. Fresh coffee, accompanied with toast and marmalade. Mama had made the coffee extra strong that morning and made sure that her daughter swallowed a little food before leaving.

"We don't want you to be sick on your first day, now do we?" Having worried a little to begin with at her daughter's new job, Mama was now quite delighted and excited at the prospect.

So, all is well, she thought. Mama seemed happy, and as she finished her breakfast, she gave her a big hug before rushing out the front door. What was in store for her? She had no idea, and her stomach churned with excitement. Would the clients like her, she wondered, never stopping to think for one moment that this job would change her entire life.

She arrived at the airport's private jet sector. The flight in question would be a two-and-a-half-hour flight. Normally on such a flight, there would only be one hostess on board, but as she was new to the job, the company had decided to give her assistance; hence a more mature hostess was assigned with her that day. The second hostess watched as she walked out of the offices and onto the tarmac, holding her briefing tightly in her right hand. She noticed a lovely girl who walked with grace and elegance, her head high, giving the impression of someone with a fair amount of experience in this field. The second hostess was also very attractive, but someone more different in looks would have been hard to find. She was very tall and ultra thin, with short blonde hair. She too looked stunning in her uniform, but the company was always very particular in their hiring of hostesses. The young ladies had to be pleasing to the eye, have an excellent memory, along with being quick and alert and adept at handling any situation, in particular with difficult customers.

As a team they all got on well, and she hoped that this newcomer would prove to be a good omen.

There were four businessmen aboard the flight that morning, all from the same telecommunications company: the CEO, the vice president of international affairs, the marketing manager, and the accountant. These four gentlemen were setting off for a business meeting scheduled for 11.30, followed by a working lunch, and a return slot had been scheduled for approximately 16.30 that afternoon. She had been warned that changes could be made at any time, as the customers' flight details were never carved in stone, albeit the majority stood by their flight time scheduling.

The pilot greeted the two hostesses, and once the formalities had been taken care of, the two girls went into the cabin to check that they had the correct food and wine that had been ordered for this short flight.

Suddenly it was time for takeoff. As she fastened her seatbelt, she gave herself a pinch and smiled across at the other hostess, who crossed her fingers and gave her the thumbs up; they both laughed as the plane took off.

The Gulfstream is not a large plane; it can accommodate up to six passengers comfortably, but today there were only four. The flight went smoothly as the gentlemen read their papers and made the occasional remark concerning that morning's news. She served them coffee and croissants. Being a morning flight, no meals or alcoholic drinks had been requested for the outbound journey.

Upon arriving at their destination, and after saying good-bye to the passengers and tidying up the cabin, she was told that she was free for the next few hours. She passed the security check and found herself within the large airport terminal. The other hostess had explained that she was taking the bus into town to meet a friend for lunch, but she had not invited her along. After wandering around looking in the airport boutiques, she also took a bus into town. She decided to buy a nice gift to take home to Mama. Perhaps some perfume or a silk scarf, something to mark this special day. She was happy to be on her own, which gave her time to think about the trip and just to be free for a little while.

She arrived back at the airport well before time; she was worried about being late and wished to make a good impression. It was better to be a little early than a little late. She had been told that timing was crucial and a top priority in this job. She ordered a coffee and read the paper she had bought in town. She then passed through Immigration and made her way to the jet. Both the pilot and the copilot were engrossed in paperwork, which she would learn later was the flight plan for the return sector.

They both said hi, and asked how she was feeling. Also they asked her if she had recovered from her first flight.

"Ready for the trip back home now?" the captain asked her.

"I certainly am," she replied as she made her way into the galley. A few moments later, the second hostess arrived, and they began sorting out bottles of wine, making sure the white was chilled and putting some champagne on ice, just in case. The caterers had provided salmon and cucumber sandwiches, cut into tiny triangles, and another tray of egg and cress, all cut wafer thin. There were also some petit fours to complete the trays, and she suddenly realised that she was hungry and could easily be tempted into tasting them. The Chrystal glasses were sparkling; now all they required were the passengers!

They finally arrived, only this time there were five of them. No introductions or explanations were given to her relating to this additional passenger, but the captain was obviously aware of this additional passenger.

Everyone took their seats, and soon they were airborne.

The return flight passed quickly. The four men from the morning all appeared to be in good spirits after what must have been an excellent meeting. They all chatted as they drank their wine and ate their way through the dainty sandwiches. At one point, she began to doubt if the caterers had supplied an adequate quantity and was glad that she had not been tempted to try a couple of them. She watched the fifth man closely and noticed that he did not speak a great deal. He neither drank the wine, nor ate any of the food on offer. Instead he had simply requested a bottle of water. He looked rather peaceful, she thought, giving him another quick glance. He was tall, rather good looking, and very suave with a tanned complexion. He was not very old; she guessed that he was perhaps in his early twenties. Rather her type, she thought, serving another passenger his wine, but she had better banish these thoughts from her mind or she would not last long in the job. She was not hired to admire or fancy the passengers.

She arrived back home, tired but happy. Mama wanted to know everything in detail, so she sat patiently and told her much of what had happened, enough to keep her happy. Mama had listened like a child being read a bedtime story and was just as excited when she opened her presents.

"You should not have spent your money like this," she had scolded her gently, but her piercing blue eyes, very like those of her daughter, could not hide her happiness.

"Now let's eat," Mama said, "then you go and have a warm bath and relax."

A little later, and now alone with her thoughts, she had time to think over her entire day. It had been one thing describing her day to Mama, but all she wanted now was to lie down and think about all the events that were turning around in her head. She knew that things had gone well and had been complimented on her first day's work; the company had told her they would be in touch soon regarding another mission. Her mind went back to the fifth gentleman who had joined the return flight; he had been so quiet, content to sit and sip his water, and had seemed to pass the time either reading or dozing. She wondered if she would see him again or if he was a regular customer. She smiled to herself as she fell asleep, still dreaming about her day.

The following week, she read a little, helped out in the house, and awaited a call for another assignment. It came on Wednesday, just as she was preparing lunch. This time, she was informed, she would be going on a five-hour trip, departing on Friday, and she was to prepare herself for a possible night stop. She was also informed that she would be flying in a Challenger.

She would be on her own for this flight, without assistance. She was not given the destination or the number of passengers, but was told that this information would be forthcoming soon.

She arrived at the airport that Friday morning and quickly went about her duties. The pilots were not the same as on the previous flight, but she was introduced to them in the VIP lounge prior to boarding the plane. Private jet crew often met for a short time prior to boarding, to discuss routes and other relevant matters before making their way onto the plane to await their passengers. This jet was considerably larger than the previous one.

"Wait until you see the interior," the copilot joked. "You will want to move in! It's like a flying hotel."

As she entered the plane, she immediately understood what he meant. The interior of the plane was opulent, designed in varying colours of beige, cream, and cappuccino. The galley had a bronze marble work top and beautiful wooden cupboards, all made to measure. No expense had been spared, she thought. Walking into the bathroom area was also a wow factor. It too was designed to please the eye. It was decorated in jade coloured marble, with a hand basin shaped like a Roman fountain. She turned on the bronze taps, and the water came cascading down. There was a variety of hand creams, soaps of all shapes and sizes, and perfumes in the beautiful hand-cut glass bottles, all from a high-class range.

She had been provided with the name of the caterer dealing with this jet; the company did not always use the same caterer, depending on the client's wishes and taste. This morning, she had received a menu consisting of caviar and finely cut smoked salmon, followed by a main meal of tournedos with a variety of vegetables. To complete the menu, there was a cheeseboard decorated with dates, figs, and grapes. She also noted that there was "*zuppa Inglese*," which she later learned was the client's favourite dessert.

Earlier she had placed a crystal bowl of fresh fruit inside the cabin, along with a bunch of the palest peach-coloured roses.

She heard the pilot call out to her that the client's limousine had arrived and was approaching the jet. A young man descended from the car and walked towards the waiting plane. As he ascended the few steps to the cabin, she realised, to her surprise, that it was the fifth gentleman, the quiet one, on her first trip.

So it was he who was travelling today, she thought, her heart beginning to race slightly more than she would have wished. It appeared that he was travelling alone, as there were no other passengers noted on her paperwork, but he would be joined by three other passengers on the return sector. So now he had a name to go with his face, a name she understood was not from this part of the world, but a name that went well with his tanned looks.

"Good morning," he said, smiling at her as she came forward to greet him. "Nice to see you again."

"You too, sir," she replied politely.

She welcomed him and invited him to choose one of the revolving armchairs. He chose a seat near the front of the cabin, on the right hand side, with another chair facing him. To his left, there was a console with a television set and a DVD recorder.

The pilot had shown her earlier that unlike the Gulfstream 150, the tables in this plane were placed on the floor and lifted up with a push of a button.

"A flying hotel," the copilot had told her, and he was far from being wrong.

She would never have believed such things possible. The trip went wonderfully well; halfway through their journey, to her great surprise, he asked her if she would care to join him for a drink. She knew that alcohol was strictly forbidden to staff on duty and therefore opted for a fruit juice; she sat down opposite him and waited for him to speak. He said very little, and she found herself asking him if everything was in order and if there was anything further he required.

"Try and relax," he answered, "and start by telling me a little about yourself."

She did not enlarge on her life but told him that she was studying to become an architect.

"So," he said, "this is just a temporary job for you." Noticing that she did not reply, he continued, "You were one of the hostesses on the plane last week, am I correct?"

"You are," she answered. "In fact, that was my first flight and this is my second."

He smiled and she did not know whether he was amused or playing with her.

"I like you," he said, "and as I have a number of trips scheduled next month, I would like you to be on board," adding, "it is always nice to see a familiar face."

Not knowing what to reply, she excused herself and told him that she had to go and prepare the meal.

"Fine," he replied, returning to his newspaper. She returned with his meal, offering him a choice of red wine with his tournedos, and was then more than happy to leave him and return to her galley, where she prepared a meal for the pilots and herself.

Over the next three months, she accompanied him on several of his trips; finally, during one trip, he asked her if she would have dinner with him that evening.

"My driver will collect you at your hotel," he told her. "Let us say around 7.30."

"That would be nice," she replied, her heart turning upside down.

"Great," he said. "I look forward to seeing you then."

As she went back to the hotel, she wondered what would be the outcome of this dinner. She had become very close to him and now began to think that her feelings were, perhaps, reciprocated. What on earth she was going to wear, she wondered. She looked around the boutiques in the hotel and found exactly what she wanted, a little black dress which was not too short but had a little bow at the back, just at the bottom of the zips. She also bought a small black clutch purse, thinking that she could hardly use her airline handbag. She smiled at the idea. She decided to wear her hair down on her shoulders, showing of its glossy shine.

She was ready half an hour earlier than planned; she took out a small bottle of white wine from the mini bar in her room and drank it straight. It helped to steady her nerves and made her more relaxed. She made her way down to the hotel entrance five minutes early but found, to her surprise, that his car was already awaiting her.

The drive to his hotel did not take more than twenty minutes, and she was happy when the journey came to an end and they reached their destination. The driver had not said very much during the journey, and she did not feel like making conversation.

She saw him waiting in the lobby of the hotel as she got out of the car. He came out to meet her and gave her a small kiss on the cheek. He told her that he had booked a table in the hotel's restaurant and hoped that she enjoyed Italian food.

The evening passed quickly and the conversation flowed, as did the champagne and the wine.

As they both drank a coffee after their meal, she wondered what was next. Would she be sent back to her hotel? The alternative, she dared not even think about.

It was he who suggested a nightcap in his room. She looked at him and quietly answered, "I would like that."

They took the lift up to his room, a rather large suite; once there, she could only gaze at the luxury. He poured them a drink and then turned towards her, lifting her face up and kissing her. She knew at this moment in time that he was attracted to her, and as his hand gently took down the zip of her dress, she suddenly felt that this was right. She was a little naive and inexperienced with men, but he led her all the way, and she soon found herself lying on the king-size bed, forgetting everything but his warm caresses. She sighed before feeling a tidal wave come over her as they began to make love.

Six months later, he asked her to marry him.

"I love you," he had told her, "and would like you to become my wife."

He had then presented her with a large square solitaire set in white gold that dazzled the naked eye. She had accepted his proposal without question and without knowing exactly what he did in life to possess money to buy such a ring.

Now, sitting in her lounge, Mama's words came flooding back, and she felt tears rolling down her check, falling like raindrops into her coffee cup.

"Can you cope with all this?" Mama had asked her. "He seems nice, but we know nothing about him or his background."

Now, twenty years later, these same words came back to haunt her, and she had a sudden longing for Mama's warm hug. Perhaps she had been right; there had been so many differences, mainly over the past five or six years. She admitted that she was unhappy, but what to do and where to go? She had become too dependent on her husband and his wealth. She had never finished her final exams to become an architect, something she often regretted.

However, she had the children, and they needed her, and somehow that was more important.

The maid came into the lounge quietly, jolting her out of all nostalgic thoughts.

"There is a telephone call for you, Madame," she said, "it is from your son's school."

She went out into the hall and picked up the phone. It was the headmaster, asking if she could come and visit him that same afternoon.

She put the phone down and made her way upstairs; as she took a shower, she wondered what the afternoon had in store for her. She thought of calling her husband at the office but decided against it. *He was also so busy, and anyway*, she thought, *I can handle the matter*, hoping that her son had not committed a serious offence.

As she dressed, her spirits rose a little. Little did she know just how much she would have to cope with in the months that were to follow.

THE GIRLFRIEND

Even to an untrained eye, she was not a beauty. She had always known this fact. Her sister was the pretty one, the one that attracted all the glances and the compliments, not that she had ever minded. She had accepted the fact gracefully and was, in actual fact, very close to her sister.

They had been orphaned when she was fifteen and her sister nineteen. Money had been tight, and although the girls' grandparents had done all they could to assist, their teenage years had not really been happy ones. Her sister had attended secretarial college, after which she had found a good job with a diamond merchant southwest of the city. She had quickly climbed the ladder of success and was eventually promoted to the position of executive assistant to the managing director.

She, on the other hand, had finished school at the age of sixteen. She had no ambitions and certainly no idea what she intended doing with her life. She knew, however, that the scope was limited without any academic qualifications. She had no wish to study or learn a trade, such as taking a secretarial course. Her sister had offered to pay for numerous training courses, but she had always declined with thanks. Instead, she preferred to work as a waitress in one of the local transport cafes, and from there, she drifted from one job to another. She knew that her sister did not approve of her lifestyle, but it suited her just fine, and she had no intention of giving it up to please anyone.

She soon had earned enough to pay for a small studio, which she furnished sparsely. She bought a bed, a table with two chairs, a sofa, and a small television. Along with, of course, the necessary items such as a fridge and a cooker which she installed in the tiny kitchen off the lounge, which also served as her bedroom. Hardly high living, but then she had few friends and never entertained.

It was not long after she bought the studio that her sister married one of the company directors, who had been transferred there eight months earlier. Her sister had asked that she be the bridesmaid at what turned out to be a rather large wedding. She had only gone out of love for her sister, and after the ceremony, followed by the usual toast to the bride and groom, she shunned the party and returned home.

That was over nine years ago, and her sister was expecting her second child in a few weeks time. She and her husband already had an adorable little girl, who had inherited her mother's blonde hair and her father's brown eyes. She loved her little niece and often babysat for the couple when they attended many of the large social functions to which they were constantly invited.

The couple were now hoping for a little boy to complete the family, but they chose not to know the baby's sex prior to the birth. The nursery was therefore prepared in a variety of colours, pale blue, lemon, and white.

One evening, her phone rang and it was her brother-in-law, asking if she would care to accompany him to a function the company was hosting in one of the city's finest hotels. He explained that her sister did not feel well enough to attend, and together they had thought she may enjoy an evening out.

Her first reaction was to refuse, but not wishing to sound ungrateful or hurt her sister in any way, she accepted the invitation. He thanked her and invited her to buy an evening gown, which would be a gift from them both.

An evening gown? She laughed and thought, *What on earth will I look like?* Her standard dress code was a pair of torn jeans, white or checked shirt tucked inside, with her hair pulled back in a ribbon. She too was blonde, but unlike her sister, it was a darker shade; a "Venetian blonde," someone had once told her, whatever that was supposed to mean.

A few days later, she went into town and, after much searching, found a dress she actually liked, much to her surprise. She tried it on and thought that it made her look different, more grown up and perhaps even a little attractive, not a word she would ever have used to describe herself. The dress was midnight blue, strapless but with hundreds of tiny shimmering stars cascading down from just under the bust to the floor. It cost a fortune, but her brother-in-law had been more than generous with the amount she had been given to spend, so she decided to purchase it straight away. She then proceeded to hunt for a pair of high heels, something she did not possess, hoping that she would be able to cope wearing them. Her choice fell on a pair of silver and blue sandals with a tiny strap around the ankle. The heel was just the right size, not too high, but they made her ankles look long and slender.

Perhaps she should think about adapting her wardrobe slightly, she thought. She liked the feeling that these luxury goods gave her, and after buying a small evening bag to match the shoes, she picked up all her parcels and caught a taxi home. She was excited as she unpacked the dress and hung it up on its silk hanger and protective cover, thus ensuring that nothing could happen to it. That evening, she tried on the dress, complete with the shoes and bag; however, as she looked in the mirror, she suddenly realised that dressing up in her home was not exactly comparable to walking into a hotel reception full of people that she had never met. By nature, she was shy, and as was her nature, she began to wonder and worry if she could go through with this event. Confidence was not a common word in her vocabulary.

The next day was the day of the function; after working all morning, she went to the hairdressers in the afternoon and decided to have her long hair put back into a chignon.

"You know," the hairdresser told her, "you should wear your hair like that more often, it suits you real well."

Later she made her way to the beautician her sister had recommended. Exhausted, she finally arrived back home and took a beer out of the fridge before slumping down on her sofa. *I have another two hours,* she told herself, *so I had better make the most of it.*

Her brother-in-law picked her up that evening; he reeled at the vision she made standing in the doorway. *So,* he thought, *the ugly duckling has become a swan.* He had had reservations at asking her to accompany him, but his wife had reassured him that all would be just perfect. How right his wife had been, he thought, taking her hand and assisting her into the taxi.

They entered the hotel foyer together, and any bystander would have thought that they made a handsome couple. It took only a moment before a gentleman in a striped grey suit walked towards them. Introductions were presented, and after a few moments of idle talk, her brother-in-law asked to be excused. The other gentleman was also called away, and suddenly, to her complete horror, she found that she was totally alone. She plucked up the courage to enter the ballroom, where all she could see was a wave of strange faces, all apparently accompanied by someone, if the laughter and chatting around the room was to be believed. She was on the verge of leaving when a voice asked if she would care for a drink. It was one of the waiters on duty that evening, and she found herself lifting a glass of champagne and putting it up to her lips.

At her side, a young man said, "Your good health; do you mind if I join you?"

"Please do," she answered, "glad of the company."

They started chatting, and the waiter reappeared to replenish their glasses.

He laid down her glass and picked up another one. She noticed that he took a second glass, presumably for himself, so he was not planning on disappearing just yet.

"Are you with someone?" he asked.

"Actually, I came with my brother-in-law, wherever he is now," she laughed, the champagne giving her a little more confidence as she felt herself beginning to enjoy the warmth of the alcohol.

"Perhaps you would care to join our table for dinner?" he asked.

She had no idea that there had been seating arrangements made for this function. She had heard her sister tell her funny stories about some of these dinners and how people actually changed seats so as not to be landed with some bore throughout the entire evening.

She hesitated, not sure what to answer. Was this young man being courteous or just feeling sorry for her? Eventually, she answered that she would love to join him at his table, and they walked across the room to take their seats. It was at this moment she saw her brother-in-law sitting at a nearby table, a blonde next to him, looking as though she was hanging on to his every word.

When he saw her, he waved her over. She pretended not to notice this gesture and turned her back in order to meet her other table guests, who were already seated.

She recognised one of the men sitting around the table, talking to a rather prominent-looking individual. More than likely an investment banker or some well-known industrialist, she thought. The gentleman she had recognised was a government minister. She had seen his picture regularly in the local papers, and he was sitting beside his lovely wife. She too was frequently in the newspapers, mainly in photos taken at the various charity functions she attended. Tonight she was wearing an evening gown in the palest shade of dust pink, with petals on both straps. She could not see the rest of the gown, as she was seated and remained that way when they had been introduced, preferring to extend a slender manicured hand. However, she had noticed the large diamond she wore on her left hand. She thought that if all the lights were suddenly to be turned off, this would give sufficient light for at least part of the dining room.

She then turned to the third gentleman sitting at the table. A tall, handsome man, in his late forties maybe, but she was sure that he was certainly not older. He spoke little but extended a warm handshake upon being introduced. He rather intrigued her. She had not quite caught his name but knew that he was not from this part of the world. He stood up to greet her, and she saw at once the quality of his attire and the immaculate articulation in his voice. His English was perfect, but she sensed this was not his mother tongue;

perhaps from attending a private school or being taught the language by a nanny? She herself was not well-educated but could perceive someone who was. Her curiosity grew.

She found herself seated between two strangers, if that is what you could name them. She had only been introduced several moments ago, and here she was, planning to pass an entire evening in their company, with very little idea of what she was going to talk about. For a moment, panic took over, and she wished that she had never accepted the invitation. She sat quietly while the starter was served. As time went by, she found that she was actually enjoying herself and had even made some of the guests laugh with stories of her little niece and other anecdotes relating to her job in the transport cafe. However, she did not add that these anecdotes were personal stories, preferring not to advertise what she did for a living or where she worked. She listened carefully as other guests related stories about the golf course and their secretaries, thus playing along with their game which to many is synonymous to socialising. The meat course soon arrived with a change of wine, and she heard someone say, as the orchestra began to play a little light music, "If music be the food of love, play on."

She laughed along with the others, having no idea why they were laughing, not knowing that this was a famous quotation and not an idle remark.

As the orchestra continued to play, she began to relax more and more. The wine had surely something to do with this effect and had perhaps gone slightly to her head. She was not used to drinking, the odd beer being more in her line. When the gentleman on her left asked if she would care to dance, she answered rather quickly that she would love to.

Her partner danced beautifully, and she soon found herself being swept around the dance floor, praying that she would not trip over her dress. She noticed that her brother-in-law was also on the floor; Barbie was now clinging to him as if her life depended on it. She made a resolution not to mention any of this to her sister. He was obviously having a good time, but then she thought of her sister alone at home, and suddenly felt angry with her brother-in-law.

The orchestra finally ceased playing and took a short break. She and her partner made their way back to the table. She noticed that the young man who had invited her to join the table was no longer present, and the other guests were now in deep conversation. Her dancing partner looked at his watch and mentioned that he had a business meeting the following day. She did not dare speak, but as he got up to leave, he discreetly handed her his business card. She took it and was about to place it in her bag when he said, "Please write down a telephone number where I can contact you."

She nervously took the pen he offered her and scribbled her mobile phone number. As he left the room, she wondered if she would ever hear from him again. Surely he had guessed how out of place she was in such surroundings.

He left the party, and she then went in search of her brother-in-law to tell him that she was ready to leave. He had been drinking heavily and could hardly manage a slurred good night. She hoped that he would make it safely home that evening and prayed that her sister would be sound asleep, thus avoiding her any heartache at seeing him in such a state.

She arrived home at around one o'clock, tired but joyfully happy. She took off her dress and hung it over the chair, kicked off her shoes, and skipped into the bathroom,

The mirror told her that her face was flushed, the result of too much wine. She cleaned her teeth and fell into bed. Just before going to sleep, she saw herself dancing in her partner's arms and wondered if he would really call her.

Three days passed, and no call was forthcoming. She kept herself very busy and visited her sister to see if she required any help. Her sister looked tired and very large, her ankles beginning to show signs of swelling. She knew that these were the last symptoms before childbirth, and she made a vow to visit her again tomorrow, and possibly take her little niece away for the day. Her sister had of course bombarded her with questions relating to the recent function, but she had said very little, preferring only to say that she had enjoyed the evening tremendously.

The following day, she arrived just as her sister's waters had broken. She stared, speechless, not sure what she should do. She picked up the phone and called an ambulance; when they arrived, she could only watch helplessly as her sister was taken away on a stretcher. She had her niece by the hand and decided that they could both do with a cool glass of lemonade while awaiting the news.

She first rang her brother-in-law at work, who said that he would go straight to the hospital.

Her nephew was born three hours later; shortly after that, her mobile rang again. She recognised her dance partner's voice immediately and felt her heart begin to race.

"How about dinner tonight?" he asked.

"I would love that," she said and then told him the good news about her sister's baby.

"Well then," he said, "we have certainly got something to celebrate. How about seven o'clock at my hotel?"

"Sounds like fun," she answered, noting down the address of his hotel.

She dressed simply, no jeans tonight. She put on a white linen shift, wore ballerina pumps, and tied her hair back in a pale blue ribbon. She threw over her shoulder a white leather bag her sister had bought her last year for her birthday and then ran into the bathroom to put on some lipstick and blush. There, looking in the bathroom mirror, she thought, *I don't look too bad*, a phrase she had never used about herself before.

He was waiting for her outside the hotel. He too was casually dressed in dark trousers and pale blue shirt open at the neck. Over his shoulders, he had thrown a navy sweater. Seeing her come out of the taxi, he walked over to greet her. He almost looked rather boyish and shy, she thought, far more than the other evening at dinner.

He had chosen a small seafood restaurant next door to the hotel. She ordered a glass of white wine and he a mineral water. He was very quiet, almost subdued, and she wondered if he was already regretting this invitation.

She was not an expert on men but had been through several rocky relationships, all of them ending rather badly; she felt somehow that this could be so different. He had made no advances, had never even tried to kiss her the other evening, so she wondered what all this was about as she sipped her drink. She noticed, like the other evening, he did not drink alcohol, preferring mineral water.

They looked at each other warily.

"Don't you drink wine?" she heard herself ask him.

"No," he said, "I prefer mineral water or fruit juice."

Never having met anyone who did not enjoy the odd drink, she was rather perplexed but said nothing. *Perhaps he is a recovering alcoholic*, she thought.

She said nothing more on the subject, and they went ahead and ordered their meal, lobster for him, whilst she chose giant prawns with a salsa sauce.

"Are you planning to stay here long?" she asked.

"Another day or so, and then it's time to set off home."

She desperately wanted to know where home was but once again hesitated in asking too many questions, afraid he would find it intrusive.

"You must be wondering why I asked you out this evening, or have you guessed?"

A difficult question, but one she knew she must answer.

"Well, I did wonder," she said, "but then thought that you may just have wanted some company while in town."

"Right so far," he continued, "but I am also very attracted to you and get the feeling that it goes both ways. Am I right?"

He saw her blush and could have kicked himself for having been so abrupt and to the point. She was a naturally lovely girl and knew nothing about his present problems at home. For a fleeting moment, he wanted to kiss her and tell her things would be just fine. But he could not do this, it would only make matters worse, he thought.

She took another sip of wine before answering him in what he could only describe as a whisper.

"Yes, you are right. I like you very much and would love to get to know you better."

"Well," he said, smiling, "why don't we start by doing exactly that? There is no time like the present."

He felt her relax and on impulse stretched his hand across the table and placed it over hers.

He knew that she was far younger than him and that she was certainly not a worldly person. He had sensed that the other evening and doubted if she had ever travelled more than a hundred miles away from this town. Perhaps it was her sweetness and unpretentious behaviour that so endeared her to him. She was so unlike the people he was accustomed to meeting; she was like a breath of fresh air in his life, and yet he hardly knew her.

He paused, still keeping his hand over hers.

He was not an impulsive man, and what he was about to tell her surprised even himself. However, he had to know if this could lead to something other than friendship. He wondered if she would be ready to hear what he had to tell her. And so he continued, "I am a married man, but an unhappy one." She looked up at him, but he noticed that she did not withdraw her hand. "I have a beautiful wife and two lovely children. My wife and I coexist. I have my business affairs, and she does more or less what she pleases. I am tired of this life and constantly having to keep up this façade. I am also a Muslim and know that there is more to life than what I am actually living."

She could only nod, trying to take everything in without looking in any way shocked or amazed at what he was telling her.

He continued, "I know very little about you, nothing in fact, but feel that somehow this can be changed, and we can look forward to some wonderful times together."

She felt completely dumfounded at his words and found that no sound would come out from her throat; she was unable to pronounce the simplest of words.

"Why don't we finish dinner and then retire up to my room?" he asked her, his eyes never leaving hers. He had to see her reaction, he had to be sure that he was right, that his decision had been the correct one.

She stared back at him, her face void of expression.

"I think I know what you mean," she said, finally speaking, adding, "Yes, let's go back to your hotel."

They left the restaurant and walked back to the hotel. They took the lift to the top floor and walked into one of the largest rooms she had ever seen. He did not give her time to speak but unzipped her dress which slid effortlessly to the floor as he began kissing her. Softly, gently at first, and soon they were in bed; the night passed in a soft passion of warmth and lust. She had never known anything like it, nor could she ever have imagined that such feeling could exist within her. She cried out the first time he entered her and found herself being overlapped with waves so strong they seemed to batter her, so much so that she held firmly to the bed post to avoid their strength bailing her over.

She found herself drowning in a sea so wild that it was only when the sun broke through the bedroom window the following morning that she knew she had weathered the storm and was still alive.

Not only alive, but very much in love.

Part II

"*All the world's a stage and all the men and women merely players. They have their exits and their entrances and one man in his time plays many parts.*"

William Shakespeare, *As You Like It, Act II, Scene 7*

THE PERSONAL ASSISTANT

She could not believe that she had actually been working in this office for over two years now.

She, who had assumed that it would just be a small part-time job, had quickly come to realise that she had been quite wrong, and in actual fact, there was a fair amount of work generated.

After working in these offices for about a month, she had been on the verge of leaving. If it had not been for the guy who ran the Public Relations department and the Investment Team on the third floor, she would have given up and handed in her notice. But they had kept her going, with their kind and cheerful manner, and so she had decided to give the job a chance . . .

The group often travelled, as did the chairman and PR manager. They both travelled together, the PR Manager dealing with all the logistics of the trips: hiring private jets, booking hotels whenever necessary, and coping with all the meeting changes (for which the chairman was notorious).

A nice job, she had often thought, travelling a jet set style, but one would need the patience of a saint to deal with what the PR position entailed. Nevertheless, with all the constant stress he was under, he often found the time to have a coffee with her, and in those moments, he would tell her about the interior of these jets, something which never failed to fascinate her. She marvelled at the idea of actually flying in one. She found herself warming to this guy, who always appeared to be so calm, cool, and collected. She knew that he was married with a little girl, and he often told her stories of how she was coping with her first months at school.

Her first year had been spent at the reception, welcoming guests and clients whilst also serving tea and coffee on the office silver. The cups and saucers were of the finest bone china, the teaspoons pure silver, and needless to add, the trays solid silver. She, who was used to dealing with CEO's and top management, had rarely seen such opulence in an office environment. Just before her first year had been completed, she began taking on some secretarial jobs for the marketing division.

Other members of staff included a chauffeur and a security officer, who also served on occasions as bodyguard to the chairman (although she felt this was slightly overdone). She found the guard a rather strange man. He could be rather boorish, had very little manners, and seemed to think that nobody but he knew the chairman. As for the new chauffeur, he was also rather arrogant and little flashy, and so she avoided them both whenever possible. She could not think why the chairman would have chosen either of them, but they both liked to refer to the important fact that they had been handpicked. A reason she had yet to fathom out, as she did not seem to understand what qualities they had that would have endeared them to "the boss," the name they gave the chairman . . . But then she remembered what he had pointed out at her interview: that he handpicked all his staff, so who was she to wonder, she asked herself.

The two men could not have been more different. The bodyguard was well over six feet tall, an impressive-looking man, but his strength appeared to be held in the pistol he wore around his waist; any intelligence he may have possessed was certainly not in his head. The chauffeur, on the other hand, was a medium-sized man in his early thirties, rather obnoxious but full of his own importance. She had often found him hovering around the reception area, trying to pick up some office gossip and chatting with the receptionist. He had the most awful habit of starting each phrase with, "I was just thinking . . ."

She hated that as much as she hated his arrogant manner and the habit he had of always putting a comb through his dark, wavy hair. She had heard through the grapevine that he could be quite a vicious person at times, one of those people where it was always wiser to be a friend than an enemy. And so she tried to get along with him, while at the same time avoiding him as much as she could. Difficult to find such a different personality to that of the chairman's old chauffeur, who had retired last year. He had been a real darling, and she regretted his absence in the office. He and his wife had moved back South, and from the news they received via the occasional postcard, they were both enjoying life to the full.

When she had started her job at the reception, she had been told that any access to the chairman was through his personal assistant, the "woman in green" who had been waiting at reception for her when she had arrived that infamous day for her interview. This lady sat in a fairly large office overlooking the water and which adjoined that of the chairman's. There was a communicating door between them, and although it was never locked, neither was it left open. It was she who took his calls and who insisted on coming down to the reception in order to meet the VIP and dignitaries who visited the office. Visitors of less importance were shown up by herself or the security guard.

"The Gates of Heaven" is what the Investment Department laughingly called the seventh floor. They had told her this jokingly one evening after work when they had invited her to join them for a drink in the bar of the hotel around the corner from the office. She had smiled upon hearing this remark, thinking of the impression she had gotten upon being taken up for her interview. Not a bad description, she had thought inwardly . . . So it had not all been in her imagination!

After she had been there for approximately eight months, she had been requested to replace the existing personal assistant. The PA was planning a few days vacation and had made a point of telling her that the chairman had specifically asked for her. Previously, they had called in a temporary lady to cover the PA's holidays or infrequent absences from the office, but this time it was she who would take over. She saw the look in the PA's face when she was being given this news and got the strangest impression that she was wondering what on earth had made the chairman ask for her.

The thought, however, pleased her. *Now I shall get a chance to see what goes on all day up there on the infamous seventh floor*, she thought.

When Monday dawned, she remembered that she had to work for the chairman for the next three days. She had not slept particularly well the previous night. Her husband had laughed and told her that all would be just fine, but she kept having visions of the instructions she had been given by the PA the previous Friday afternoon: green tea in the morning, with a glass of mineral water, the weather chart to be placed on his desk. Plus the fact that she should remember to place the tea and water on the silver tray which had been cut to measure and inserted on the right-hand side of his desk. All this, plus those burning brown eyes, would no doubt put her off for the entire three-day period.

She, who had worked with top management all of her professional career, knew that she was good, in fact amongst the best in town, but when it came to this CEO and his strange manners, she was not so sure. Over breakfast with her husband, she began to worry in case the tea was too strong or she chose the wrong type of water or forgot to use the silver tray. Perhaps he would ask for coffee or a different type of mineral water. She burst out laughing when her husband told her that she was becoming paranoid! She arrived earlier than usual that Monday in order to giver herself plenty of time to prepare all she had been requested to do.

Suddenly her phone rang, and it was the chairman, advising her that he was ready to be collected and to inform the chauffeur.

She then phoned the chauffeur, who surprisingly asked her, "Where do I have to meet him?"

"To hell with him," she said to herself under her breath. She had just spoken with the CEO, and he had reiterated that he should be collected at the usual place, which she had taken to be the villa.

So they were trying to make her appear stupid, she thought; well, she would show them. She called back the chauffeur and told him that he should make his way directly to the villa, knowing very well that was what he was doing. From the silence at the other end of the line, she knew that she had been right. So far, so good, she thought, deciding to go and make herself an espresso and enjoy a moment's relaxation before everyone arrived. She then called the security to advise them that the chairman was on his way and should be there in around ten minutes. This was the pattern she had learned; the guard would meet the chairman and accompany him up to his office, where she would be waiting to greet him.

Finally, he arrived and she heard the guard unlocking his office door. Moments later, she heard the chairman trying to enter her office through the adjoining door. She had been in his office earlier, with the morning's papers and, of course, the weather chart. She sat tight and waited. A few moments later, he arrived from the corridor and stood at her office door.

"Are you frightened of me?" he asked her, smiling.

"No, not at all," she replied.

"Then why have you locked the adjoining door?"

"Your PA told me to keep it locked," she answered truthfully.

"So, how about opening it, and in this way, we can see one another, unless you have any objection?"

She wondered if he was mocking her but answered politely, "None whatsoever."

Oh my God, she said to herself, *what else was I told that was not completely truthful?*

Now he is going to ask me for a latte or a milky coffee rather than his green tea, she assumed, smiling.

True to her thoughts, he asked for a latte and a glass of water.

"Tell me," he asked her, "when do you plan to go to lunch?"

She had decided not to make any luncheon engagements for the few days that she working for him, as his PA had warned her that she should always be around, in case she was required, and only when she was told could she go for lunch.

"Around one o'clock," she heard herself say.

"Fine," he answered. "Take your time. Now let's get the coffee and have a look through the mail."

She could not believe what she was hearing; he almost sounded human. So all went well the following days, and soon she found herself replacing his assistant on a regular basis, whenever she was away. To say that she and the chairman had become friends would be a slight hyperbole, but they got on just fine.

A few months later, in a total surprise to everyone, his PA decided to leave her position, having met an elderly widower whom she planned to marry. She was asked if she would like the position on a permanent basis; the chairman had told her that he thought she was the best person to take over.

"Your contract and salary will, of course, be changed," he had told her, "and I know that you will do your best to fulfil this position."

"Perhaps," she had answered, "but may I take a couple of days to think it over and discuss things with my family?"

"Fine," he had replied. "I shall be expecting your answer shortly," adding that he would be more than happy if she did decide to accept his proposition.

She got up, they shook hands, and she left the room smiling. She knew that she would accept his offer but was not ready to let him know so quickly. She had mentioned her family to buy time; it had been a bluff, but one she hoped he had not picked up.

She soon settled down to the routine and found, to her surprise, that she really enjoyed the new job. She tried to make the chairman a little more accessible to the staff, a change which meant that he got to see them more often; he started going around the office each morning to shake hands with the staff. Somehow this gave the office a more relaxed tone, and the staff began to acknowledge the fact that he could be receptive to some of their suggestions concerning work. Several changes were made, and she felt pleased that she had been partly responsible for many of them.

The chairman was not a demanding man, although he liked his own way. He was meticulous in many of his mannerisms. She kept his diary, always knowing his whereabouts; he did not like anyone knowing his plans in advance and so discretion was a top priority. She soon got to know many of the dignitaries who visited, and when she saw the boardroom where these meetings took place, she was totally amazed. The room must have been twelve by twenty metres, set up with videoconferencing and all possible technical equipment imaginable. The conference table which sat in the middle of the room was extremely long, with the possibility of seating twenty people.

Within the room there were four large wooden doors, two leading out to the corridor, one directly into the chairman's office, and the other cleverly designed to lead into the kitchen, where the receptionist could prepare the tea and coffee to be served during the meetings.

There were several beautiful paintings hanging on the wall. Two were by the French painter Dunoyer de Segonzac and another painting she recognised to be a Picasso. She wondered if these wonderful paintings were originals. She particularly loved the Dunoyer de Segonzac aquarelles. The one entitled, *Nature morte au melon* was her favourite. This painting depicted flowers, with a melon sitting on a dish, a glass siphon and a plate of lemons. Underneath this plate was the French newspaper, *Le Provencale*. She often thought this was so chic and French, as was the other painting hanging beside it, entitled *Le Panama et le Figaro*.

Each Monday, three bouquets of flowers were delivered to the office. One colourful bouquet was placed at the reception area, the second bouquet was for the chairman's office, and the largest bouquet was for the boardroom. This bouquet, she noticed, was always made up of roses in the palest shade of pink.

This week, they were receiving a delegation from one of the African states along with an ambassador from one of Europe's southern countries. As was customary, the chauffeur, the guard, and the chairman's PR had gone up to the airport to meet them and drive them back; they always used either the Rolls Royce or the Bentley, depending on the number of visitors.

She remembered riding in the Bentley when she had attended a dinner dance function, and it was there that she had met the chairman's wife. She had assisted in planning the dinner, and it had been a great success. At one point in the evening, she found herself sitting at a table, across from her boss's wife.

"What a beauty," she had thought at the time, admiring her style, not to mention her incredible blue eyes. She was so natural and easy to make conversation with, and by the end of the evening, they had promised to meet up in the near future for lunch.

"Give me a call soon," the chairman's wife had told her, giving her a telephone number where she could be reached.

The following week, the chairman had made a point of telling her that his wife had enjoyed meeting her, to whom she replied, "I did too, and she really is a lovely person."

She noticed that he now had placed a silver frame on his desk near his phone. The picture showed the chairman and his wife, laughing, and had been taken at the function the previous week. Certainly a marriage made to last, she thought. They went so well together; he, with all his trappings of wealth, could have chosen anyone, but she was happy to see that he had chosen the best and appeared to know this fact.

She was therefore a little surprised when a couple of weeks later, just as she was tidying up for the day and preparing to go home, that the chairman's wife appeared in her office. They chatted over a fruit juice, mainly about the children, the latest skirt lengths, and other trivial matters.

They decided there and then to meet up for lunch the following Wednesday at a nearby hotel.

It was then that the chairman appeared and told his wife that it was time to leave, and that the chauffeur was awaiting them. For one split second, there had been a slight chill in the atmosphere, as if a blast of cold air had somehow entered the room through the closed window. They left, and she thought for a moment about what she had just felt; she told herself it was nonsense before proceeding to put on her camel coat, lifting up her handbag, and making her way to the lift. The sun was shining as she left the building, and she wondered what on earth had given her the impression of being cold. *My imagination runs wild sometimes,* she thought, laughing, as she ran to catch the bus.

As arranged, the two ladies met the following week at one of the modern hotels located near the office. It had a lovely terrace overlooking the water and was just perfect to relax and chat. She had asked for the entire afternoon off, knowing that an hour would be insufficient and she did not wish to hurry back to the office. There was also the other factor of not broadcasting to the office where she was going; hence taking the afternoon off gave her time to enjoy her own time. After studying the menu, they both chose melon for starters followed by a fish dish. She noticed that her friend chose to drink water and not wine. As it was warm, she decided to choose water also. She wondered if, like her husband, she was a nondrinker but hesitated about asking her. It was rather pretentious and, after all, none of her business. Just before choosing the dessert course, her friend's phone rang.

The chairman's wife answered her mobile and could be heard to say, "You know that I am having lunch with your secretary, I told you last night."

Very few other words were spoken and the subject was not raised. The PA half expected her phone to ring now, but it did not. The dessert arrived, but her appetite had vanished. They continued talking, but in some way, the call had put a damper on things. Could it be that he was overly possessive with her, the PA wondered. Surely not, but something was not quite right.

Perhaps they were going through a difficult patch in their marriage, as all couples do, but sometimes there could be a more serious situation, differences that went far deeper, far away from the arguing over hours spent at the office or about the kids, differences that were never heard but which they preferred to remain silent about.

"Let's get the bill," the PA said, "have coffee in the city centre and catch up on the new perfumes."

She was rewarded with smile, and so they set off. At around five o'clock and after a little window shopping, they said good-bye and promised to keep in touch.

"I really like you," the chairman's wife said, hugging her.

"Thanks, you know, I rather like you too and I believe that we are going to get along just fine."

Her husband was presently away on a long haul trip, and was not expected home until later that week. When he rang later her that evening, she told him about her afternoon.

"It sounds as though you had a really good time," he said.

"You know, honey," she replied, "I really did."

The next morning, she awoke early and dressed carefully in a black pencil skirt and a beige jacket with large gold buttons; underneath, she wore a black lace camisole. To this, she added a string of pearls and earrings and slipped into a pair of high-heeled beige court shoes.

She arrived as usual at the office and went about her tasks before making a coffee.

The boss arrived around ten o'clock and seemed to be in good spirits.

"How are you today?" he asked. "Did you enjoy your luncheon date with my wife?"

"Very much," she answered, not giving any other information.

He said no more on the subject but added that he was planning a large function for several VIPs and wanted her to work with his PR manager closely to ensure that the event ran smoothly and according to plan. The bid for the hedge fund had gone through without a hitch, and this was now to be the second event the company planned in order to promote their strategy and future investments.

He also asked that she invite her husband to the event, saying that he looked forward to finally meeting him.

"Book a nice double room for both of you," he added, "so that you can enjoy the evening and stay over until Sunday."

She knew that her husband was not on duty that weekend and was thrilled that he would at last be able to join her and meet the chairman and the rest of her colleagues.

The event was a highly successful. The speeches were excellent, the food was wonderful, and the guests made no effort to hide their enjoyment at attending such a weekend event. She had also organized a spa on Saturday afternoon for the wives attending the function, something which they seemed only too pleased to participate.

She had been happy to meet up with her boss's wife again. She looked radiant at the dinner on the Saturday evening, dressed in a red cocktail dress with a sequined bolero top. She wore very high silver heels and was at her most charming. So her doubts had been about nothing, she told herself. The couple once again looked the perfect duo as they welcomed everyone and danced the night away. Her husband had enjoyed the evening tremendously, and she noticed that he had spent quite a fair amount of time speaking to the chairman and many of the guests. He was always at ease in company, and everyone was always interested the moment he told them that he was an airline pilot. They had been able to have a little while together prior to the dinner, which meant they had the opportunity to dance and mix with guests. The outcome being, they had both found the weekend to be more relaxing than they could have ever expected. Later that evening in their room, her husband had told her that she was very lucky to hold such a position and that he had found her colleagues to be interesting, her boss charismatic, and his wife, well, "just too beautiful" were his exact words.

So, she thought that night lying in bed once her husband had fallen asleep, her worries were about nothing. Well, she thought before falling asleep, all is well and there is nothing to worry about.

The following week was quiet, mainly due to the recent busy schedule leading up to the event and the fact that the chairman was away on a business trip. For once, she found herself with little to do and, at the same time, feeling a little drained.

"What I need is a holiday," she had told the receptionist that morning. "I shall have to be extra nice to my husband and ask him to take me away on an exotic break for a few days."

She was just about to make herself a pot of tea when the phone rang. It was the chairman's wife, asking if she was free for lunch the following day.

"Sure," she replied. "Give me a time and where you want us to meet."

"Let's go to the new Italian restaurant in the old town," she said. "It's supposed to be very good, and I need to get out of the house."

They fixed a time and just before saying good-bye, she suddenly asked, "Is my husband away the entire week?"

The PA hesitated a second before answering, "Why yes, he is expected back on Saturday; that is the schedule I have been given, but I can check it out with his PR manager."

"No, please don't bother," now she added.

The next day, they met at La Fenice and both ordered Crespelle followed by Saltimbocca for her friend and a steak Florentine for herself. It was during the main course that her friend opened up:

"You know, I think my husband is having an affair."

The PA looked at her, aghast.

"Whatever makes you think that?" she asked.

"Just a feeling I have had for a few months now. Have you by any chance heard any rumours about such a thing?"

"To be honest I have not, but then would I?"

"Do you have any idea who the person might be?"

"Not really, but I have my suspicions that it could be one of the air hostesses, and I should know all about that," she added with a faint smile. "Or maybe just someone he has met on one of his numerous trips."

There was a silence between them, the PA not daring to say or add anything further at that precise moment in time. Her friend was hurting, and she had no idea how to comfort or reassure her that all was well, even though she had heard nothing about an affair. The waiter was a welcome break, and as they ordered their espressos, the cloud over the table lifted, as they spoke of her daughter's eventual move to the States, where she had been offered a job as a trainee/ apprentice in a fashion magazine.

Before departing, she asked the PA to let her know if she heard anything pertaining to her husband having an affair. "You know offices are always rife with rumours," she said, "and if there is anything going on, then I am sure you will finally hear about it."

"Of course," she had answered, "but don't get too concerned, I am sure there is nothing to worry about." They then proceeded to pay their bill and left the restaurant out into the warm June sunshine.

"Fancy a walk in the park?"

"No," the wife said, "I think I shall go home now and get some rest. I did not sleep very well last night. However, I shall be in touch soon, and we can get together for another bite to eat."

She waved as her friend walked down the road and she set off to return to the office. On her way up to the seventh floor, she bumped into the chauffeur. She took the opportunity of asking him when he had to collect the chairman at the airport.

"Saturday" he replied. "Why? Have there been any changes?"

"No," she replied. "I was just checking."

"Well, you keep the diaries," he told her. "Don't you have a copy of his itinerary?"

"Sure I do, I just wanted to check what time you planned on being at the airport." She blushed, cursing herself for asking him too many questions. She turned as if to finish the conversation and made her way up to her office. Quite an eventful day, she thought.

There were a couple of messages for her and she was happy to keep her mind occupied.

Later that afternoon, she thought over the lunch conversation. Was it possible that her boss was having an affair, and if so, with whom? She would try to speak to the PR manager next week; if anyone knew something, then it would be he. However, she would have to be very discreet and not raise his suspicions. Even if he knew anything, it was unlikely that he would confide in her. The rest of the afternoon passed quickly, and just as she was preparing to leave, the phone rang; it was the chairman.

"There has been a slight change to my programme," he told her. "I shall not be arriving until later tomorrow evening and will go directly to a dinner engagement in town. Please advise my chauffeur and tell him that his services will not be required until later."

"Fine," she said. "Do you wish me to make dinner reservations?"

"No thanks," he replied quickly. "I shall take care of things myself."

She brought him up to date on his calls and a meeting she had set up for him the following week with one of the private banks.

"Great," he said, "so have a good weekend, and we shall see each other on Monday morning."

Putting on her jacket, she glanced once more around the office before telling the guard that he could now close up the offices for the evening. She took the lift down and waved to the receptionist as she left the building.

Alone in bed later that evening, she pondered over her day and wondered if it could be possible that the chairman was having an affair. How could his wife think such a thing if there was not some truth in the matter? She fell asleep before finding an answer to her question.

THE MISTRESS

They had continued their liaison for a year. She did not see him that often, but he kept in touch by phone, and they always managed to spend a few days together each month when business brought him to her part of the world.

Nobody knew about this love affair. She had not dared tell her sister, knowing that she would disapprove of her seeing a married man, and as she had few friends to confide in, the matter remained a secret. The secret, however, was known to one person: the PR manager.

She had been totally taken aback upon being introduced to the PR manager. He had invited her to join his table that evening a year ago when she had attended the function with her brother-in-law; without him, she would never have met her lover. They both got on well together and he was always there whenever necessary. She knew that he had the confidence of the chairman and that the affair would never go past his ears. He was happily married with a little girl of five, and he often amused her with stories of her latest antics.

"Don't you mind being away from home so much?" she had asked the PR manager once when they were sitting having a drink in the foyer of the hotel where they were staying.

"I do," he had replied, "but it's my job. My wife has an excellent job also, which means that she is not too alone during the day when the little one is at school. However, if things could be different, I would rather be with them right now, but that is impossible, so why worry over things we cannot change?"

"Have you told her about me?" she asked.

"No," he answered quietly. "I think it wiser that this matter be kept quiet, don't you agree?"

She pondered a moment before adding, "Do you think that his wife suspects anything?"

"That is a question only one person can answer, and that person is not me."

She remained silent, feeling rather awkward and stupid at having asked him these questions.

"You know that I am in love with him."

"Are you, or do you just think that you are?" he replied rather more dryly than he meant to.

"No, I really do love him and believe that he loves me, at least a little."

The PR, not wishing to delve any deeper into such a subject, was relieved to see his boss arrive at this point in time. They chatted briefly, and the PR then left them in the lobby to go up to his room.

Once there, he showered and thought back on her questions; if the truth be known, he too had been wondering where this relationship was going to end. He knew the chairman's wife well, liked her very much, and could not completely fathom out why this particular affair was continuing. It quite intrigued him as he found the young girlfriend to be quite plain and not overly intelligent, at least to him; such a contrast to the chairman's wife, who was charming, witty, and above all so pretty.

However, he had to admit that with her innocent look and quiet determination to please, she appeared to be keeping his boss interested. Whether this would be enough to break up the marriage, he doubted, but the affair had now lasted over a year, and he wondered what the outcome would be.

He remembered that it had been mentioned bringing her over to Europe on one of the return trips, something he did not think was a good idea, but he had remained silent at the time. It was after all none of his business, and he knew that his boss always got his own way in the end and no doubt would bring up the matter with him again. He silently prayed that he would have sense to tell his wife about his affair, before bringing his mistress home on a trip.

And so it was that a few days later, he received a call from the chairman advising that there would be one more passenger on the flight returning the following evening and requesting that he prepare the necessary documents. He shuddered at the thought.

She hated herself for having asked the PR all these questions. Of course he did not know what to reply. How could he? The fact was simply that she was very much in love and had thought by probing a little, her only friend may have given something away. She had been so wrong.

Her lover had promised to take her away several times, but so far he had not mentioned it again. He had told her that he would set her up in a little flat pending the separation from his wife. She did not even dare think of such a thing. Was he really ready to give up his family for her? He told her that was what he wanted and that he was happier with her than he had been for a long time. However, she knew very well that from there to giving up a family and a wife he had been married to for twenty-two years was another matter. She knew that he was immensely rich and that he was of Muslim faith; he neither smoked nor drank, but this did not bother her. He had on one occasion asked her to give up smoking and drinking beer. She had been rather taken aback but had stopped smoking, at least in front of him. When he left, she resumed her habits, which were after all her only comfort for all the weeks that he was away.

She knew little about religion; in fact, she did not even know if she had been baptised. She had been at her niece's christening, but that was special. She had been the godmother and had held the baby in church during the baptism. As for Islam, she knew nothing on the matter and avoided the subject. He travelled with a praying carpet, and she had seen him on several occasions kneeling in their hotel suite. She had always left him alone at this moment, leaving him to pray and recollect his thoughts in total peace and privacy.

A more educated girl would have delved into some of the religious aspects of the Islamic faith and perhaps learn or understand some of its concepts. This had never occurred to her. She accepted him exactly as he was. He was good to her, brought her presents, and invited her out to the best restaurants. He had even given her an account with one of the best stores, telling her to buy herself some pretty dresses and "perhaps shoes with a heel."

"You cannot always go out with pumps and gym shoes," he had told her on one of his visits.

So, she had invested in a few simple but stylish short linen shift dresses. As she was fairly tall and slim, these dresses suited her well. She still kept her hair in the same style, either tied back in a ribbon or hanging loosely on her shoulders. She rarely wore makeup, perhaps a touch of gloss and some blusher. Anything else was not really her style.

Not wishing to raise her sister's suspicions by suddenly appearing with a complete new wardrobe, she kept her clothes mainly for his visit, and he seemed pleased with the change in her appearance.

The PR started dealing with the necessary documents for the return flight. This was not a great problem for him, as he knew that the jet could take another passenger without any problem and that the luggage would be minimal, but what about the repercussions, he thought. He advised the pilot and the caterers to provide an additional meal on board the return flight.

She jumped with joy when he announced to her that she would be leaving the following evening. She hugged him and cried with joy, and then she paused. "What am I going to tell my sister?" she asked him.

"Just tell her that you are planning a few days holiday. You don't need to tell her everything you do," he had advised her.

Everyone takes a break now and again, he had said, and so she did just what he had suggested. It never entered her head to do anything else. Her sister was happy for her, but she noticed that she did not ask too many questions. She was in the middle of feeding the baby when she rang to tell her about her imminent departure, as well as attempting to watch her favourite television series, and so no awkward questions were asked, and she told her that she would see her soon and to give the children a big hug.

That done, she turned to packing a small suitcase with a few dresses, a pair of jeans, some shoes, and other small essentials. She had been told to travel light, and this suited her fine.

The following evening, she came on board, and as it was a night flight, dinner was served rapidly. There was little conversation, the others on board being rather eager to settle down for the night. The jet had a resting area to the rear of the plane, and after a light dinner, they both retired there to rest. She was tired and fell asleep quickly, the excitement of the past forty-eight hours being too much for her. When she awakened, it was pitch dark.

Where am I? she asked herself, before remembering. He was sleeping at her side, and she did not feel inclined to move, in case she wakened him. She would have loved to go to the bathroom but decided that she could wait a little longer in order that he may continue resting.

She was excited about arriving in Europe for her first trip abroad; their destination sounded magic, with its lakes and mountains. She could not wait to arrive.

The chairman moved and opened his eyes.

"Are you already awake?" he asked her.

"I am too excited to sleep, and I think that we are about to have breakfast. I can smell the coffee."

She had heard movement in the front cabin and smelt the aroma of freshly brewed coffee and warm bread wafting through the plane. She went to the bathroom, washed her face, brushed her teeth, and slid on a clean shirt before joining the rest of the group for breakfast. She had noticed all the perfumes and soaps on display but left these behind, such was her excitement to hurry to the main cabin for breakfast and take in the view, now that dawn was approaching. This was something she did not wish to miss, never having flown before. Now, in the daylight, she saw that the main cabin had huge leather armchairs that swivelled around and which could also lean downwards to make a sort of bed, or more a sleeping chair. She had been too excited last evening to take in all these things, but this morning she noticed every detail, from the flowers, the soft music, and now the news being broadcast over a plasma television. *Oh my God,* she said to herself, almost out loud, *this is fantastic, and what a way to travel.* There were small tables laden with orange juice, fresh fruit, little cream-coloured coffee pots, and pretty flowered napkins.

She thought of the cafes where she worked and thought, *This must be the other side of life.*

The hostess served her a coffee and poured into her cup some warm milk. She was then offered a selection of toast, croissants, and other dainty pastries. She looked around the cabin and watched how the others put up their tables, preparing also for their morning snack.

An hour later, it was time for landing, and she felt her heart flutter and the butterflies tightened in her stomach as they prepared for touchdown.

She knew that she was going to be staying in a hotel in the city centre for a few weeks before moving into an apartment near the office. It was presently being redecorated for her, and this would be her home for the following months.

"I have to sort things out, my love," he had told her. "Just bear with me for a month or so, and then everything will be fine."

She thought that she also had some sorting out to do, especially where her sister was concerned, but she put that thought out of her head, at least for now. This was not the time to think of anything else but the present moment in time.

The jet landed, and they were met by Immigration and Customs control. The guy from PR seemed to know everyone and everything. Soon they were in the arrivals hall, where a smallish man wearing a navy suit awaited them.

"Good morning," he said to the chairman. "I hope that you had a good flight."

"Fine," he answered. "By the way, you have both cars here at the airport, don't you?"

"Yes," he replied.

"I shall take my own," the chairman said, "as I have things to attend to in town. You take our guest to the bank and drop my PR manager at the office; he has some papers to collect. Then drive him straight home, as he needs a good rest."

The party split up in the arrival hall, but before departing, the chairman told the other gentleman, "I shall see you tonight for dinner, but let's not make it too late. Let me give you a call later this afternoon when we have all rested, and we can fix a time and place."

"Fine," the banker replied. "I shall await your call."

She followed on without having been introduced to either the banker or the chauffeur. She and the chairman got into a huge blue car, whilst the others drove off in what she thought was a Range Rover, although she was not certain.

Soon they were at the hotel, and after checking in, he took her up to show her around. The room was in actual fact one of the hotel's finest suites, complete with large bay windows which looked directly on to the marina, where guests could admire the luxurious yachts moored. To the other side of the room there was a large window where it was possible to see a huge church spiral, which she was told was that of the city's cathedral in the old part of the town. It was not too far away from the hotel and, on a nice day, well worth a stroll up the cobbled streets which were full of art galleries and bistros.

The suite was decorated in all shades of Bordeaux, pink, and beige. The en-suite was the colour of Indian rose marble with grey edgings along the bath and the shower. There was a Jacuzzi and two huge wash hand basins. At each side there was a little pink basket of dried rose petals and a selection of perfumes, divine-smelling soaps, and all sizes of towels in varying shades of pink and grey, some of them so large they could have been small carpets. There was also a selection of hand towels hung around the bathroom, the smallest being white edged with pink and grey lace. A huge mirror hung on the wall with lights around the top, something an actress would have in her room, she thought to herself, thinking back on the odd time she and her sister had gone to the movies when they were younger.

"It's just fantastic," she told him.

"I am glad that you like it," he said, smiling at her. He had been watching her reaction to the hotel room; she had been like a child opening up presents. This childlike innocence was one of the reasons he loved this slip of a girl so and was ready to give her all he possibly could in order to make her happy. His wife had been like her when they had first met, he thought suddenly. She too had understood him at one time, but now, he was not so sure about this fact. He felt suddenly a little guilty, thinking of his lovely wife. He still thought of her often and had no idea how he was going to ask her for a divorce. He tried to persuade himself that perhaps she would be relieved that finally the truth was out, but deep down he was not so certain that this was true.

He knew his wife was spoilt and volatile, but then this was partly his fault. He had made her like this. She had been a completely different person when they had first met. Nothing had been good enough for her, and he had loved her more than life itself, and she too had once loved him that way, of that he was certain. Over the past four or five years, things had changed; she had become distant. He knew he had become deeper involved with his religion. She had never converted to Islam, and he had never asked her to.

He was still not sure where things would lead with this young girl. "Love" was a big word, and in his own way he did love her. However, a divorce was going to cost him dearly, and he was not entirely certain that was what he really wanted. He knew his wife only too well; the next few weeks were not going to be an easy ride.

What he did not know at this specific moment was the fact that his wife already had serious doubts about his having a liaison and just how much sorrow and financial ruin would come out of the entire affair. He would learn soon enough.

The PR Manager

He had always liked and respected his boss, a kind and generous man who liked to make all his own decisions, which he had to admit at times could be difficult, to say the least. The chairman liked his own way, that was sure, and he had realised that from day one. They had never actually argued, although they had often come fairly close, but he preferred to give in and let the boss have his own way, rather than make life more difficult for himself. The salary was excellent, and he knew that flying around the world, often on private jets, and staying in the best hotels could not be a better way to make one's living! The job was a demanding one and took him away from home a great deal. This part he was not too keen about, as he often worried about leaving his wife and five-year-old daughter at home alone. However, his wife held an excellent position within a telecommunications company, her hours were flexible, and she was the perfect mother to their little daughter.

He missed them both right now, his wife, with her flame-coloured hair complete with its unruly curls, the freckles on the bridge of her nose which spread across her cheeks in the summertime, and her bright green eyes, almost the colour of the sea on a windy day. His little daughter was very much like his wife and had the same colouring, although her eyes were the colour of sand, a bit like his own. He loved them very dearly and perhaps never told them of this fact. He made up his mind there and then to let them both know this, once he returned from this trip.

His boss was also a great family man, something they both had in common. That was true until about a year ago, when things had changed, and unfortunately, not for the better. He knew that the chairman was having an affair, quite a serious one he felt, although he knew very little about it. The affair had been continuing for some time now, and he was not sure how things were going to turn out. It was not that it bothered him; he just felt that it was so unlike the man he knew and respected.

His mind went back about a year ago, remembering only too well that particular evening when, on one of their longer business trips, he had met this young girl in the hotel lobby. She had looked so lost and alone, that he had, on impulse, invited her to join their table. It was then that she had met the chairman, and it appeared to him that the affair had started that evening.

The following day, the chairman had requested him to book a chauffeur-driven car for ten o'clock in the evening, but he had said nothing further. This had rather surprised him, for his boss was known to retire early; he was not someone who had the habit of going out on his own without giving his whereabouts. Furthermore, he had been handed a bundle of notes and told to go out and enjoy himself.

The PR manager had worked most of his life in the airline industry. Eleven years with a large commercial company as sales manager, after which he had taken over as airport manager. It was then that he had met the chairman, one of the company's treasured customers, a prominent client who had once told him, "If you ever decide to change jobs, let me know."

A year later, he had done just that and had never once regretted his decision. Not until this moment, he thought. He felt as if he had been given a payoff and did not particularly relish the feeling.

Knowing that he would be dining on his own that evening, he decided to eat at the hotel's Italian restaurant, where he treated himself to pasta ai funghi, followed by some very tender veal cutlets. He ordered a small bottle of Barolo and finished off the meal with a Vecchia Romagna. He enjoyed the meal but wished that his wife could be with him to share the fine dining.

To be fair, the chairman had asked him on many occasions to bring his wife along on some of their trips, but she never came. She always had a reason for not flying with them, and so he had finally ceased asking.

He had told his wife many stories of the receptions and functions he had attended; she only smiled and laughed at many of his anecdotes, never showing any signs of jealousy. He knew that she was happy with her lovely home and her "Americans," as she called her superiors in the States, who were always happy to visit their home when they were in Europe. She had been on more than one occasion to visit the head office and had enjoyed her trips tremendously, almost making it sound like fun. But then that is just her nature, he thought. She was quick and clever, never taking herself or life too seriously. A born optimist, unlike himself, who took life perhaps too seriously and who had a habit of looking on the black side rather than laughing things off. But that is why they got on so well; they made a good team, their differences sometimes leading to arguments, but they were happy and he prayed that nothing would ever change that. Their little daughter complemented their happiness, and he could not have wished for anything more in life.

If the truth be known, he was not entirely sure that his wife completely trusted his boss.

"Where does he make all that money?" she had once asked him. "What sort of lucrative business is he in to make that sort of money?"

The questions had angered him as he quickly rose to defend the chairman. Yet, on afterthought, he had to give her some credit. He did not know either where his wealth came from, and to be fair, she had every right to ask the question. Had the new PA not asked him the same question a few months back?

He decided to go for a stroll around the garden before turning in for the night, and then he remembered that there was to be another passenger travelling with them on the return leg the next evening. He had a strong idea that it was the young lady he had invited to join their table the previous year at one of their functions. He had felt sorry for her then but could never have guessed that this meeting was to be the start of an affair which had now lasted almost a year. The boss had told him that he had promised to bring her over to Europe on one of their return trips, an idea he did not entirely approve of, but then it was not his business. He had the logistics to sort out, and that was enough for him to deal with.

The following afternoon, they all assembled at the airport. As was customary, he was always there an hour prior to departure, ensuring that all the administrative work was complete and the flight plan signed off prior to the passengers arriving.

He saw the car arrive, and as she got out of the car, he knew at once that it was she. He had gotten to know her pretty well over the past year, a coffee and a cigarette now and then, when time permitted, and furthermore he knew that she was in love with his boss. She had confided this fact to him several months earlier. So, he had finally decided to bring her back with him on this voyage. Well, plenty of questions are going to be asked, he thought whilst walking across to the car to meet them.

"Hello," she said, smiling. "How nice to see you again."

The chairman looked on, saying nothing, other than a few words to a couple of business associates who were travelling with them that evening.

Finally, after what seemed like an eternity, the chairman asked him if all the paperwork had been completed, to which he replied that all was in order and that they could all now board.

"The crew are waiting to welcome you," he told him.

"Then let's all get on board and take off."

The PR manager felt rather uneasy when, several minutes later; he climbed the few steps into the plane himself and the door closed behind him.

The following week is going to be something else, he thought to himself. *How the hell is this news going to be kept secret?*

However, his questions would soon be answered, perhaps even sooner than even he imagined.

THE COFFEE BREAK

His main concern returning home was that it would not be too long before someone in the office asked a question about the "new arrival." Rumours ran like forest wildfires, and he had no doubt that someone would begin to put two and two together.

He was therefore not surprised when the PA rang him on his first morning back at the office.

"Hi," she said. "I have a spare moment if you would care for a coffee."

"Sure," he replied. "I could do with some company; give me a couple of minutes and I'll come up to your office."

As she waited for him, she pondered how she was going to bring up the subject. It was a delicate one, and knowing the PR as she did, she knew that he was very discreet about all the business trips he undertook with the chairman; this was not going to be easy. He was soon in her office, as promised.

Now was her chance, and she went straight for it.

"How do you spend your evenings when you don't have dinner and functions to attend?" she asked him innocently.

She saw him hesitate slightly and she poured out his coffee as they chatted about their respective families.

"How did your last trip go?" she asked quietly. "You certainly had your hands full with all the meetings and functions that were scheduled on this trip. Did you manage to have some time to yourself?"

"Tell me about it," he answered.

Now was her chance; she went straight in.

"How do you spend your evenings?" she asked him again.

"Oh," he said, "I go out to the local bistros, taste the local food and wine whenever I get the chance, and you know what? I actually enjoy these evenings."

"And what about the boss?" she continued. "Does he always join you in these relaxing evenings?"

"Well, certainly not regarding the wine tasting," he laughed, "but he does sometimes join me, and he always seems to fit in; you know what he is like. He is not that difficult."

However, he added, "He's a pretty quiet guy, as you well know, and so I often find myself on my own or with the security guard if he is with us on the trip, but believe me, I can enjoy my own company; I need it."

"Could you imagine him having an affair while he is away?" She hated herself for making such a remark and putting the poor guy in such a spot, but she had to know.

"Why would you ask me such a question?" he asked her, looking at her with surprise.

"Oh, I don't know, forget what I said, it was not very appropriate. I'm truly sorry," she added. "It's just that I had lunch with his wife last week, and she seems convinced that he is having an affair with one of the air hostesses. To be honest, she seemed really concerned and seems convinced that there is someone else in his life. I thought if anyone would know, it would be you; you are both so close, and you always travel with him."

He sat without any comment.

"I'm sorry for what I said now," she told him. "Forgiven? Let me fill up your cup, and please forget anything I said."

She left her office, and he was glad of the interlude. It gave him time to think of what he was going to tell her and how much he could say in confidence. He liked and trusted her, and she might as well know. In this way, he would not be the only one carrying around the burden. She would be discreet, of that he had no doubt, and as she was close to the chairman's wife, he thought it wiser to keep her advised of the situation. She did have the right to know what was going on, even for her friend's sake.

She came back into the office carrying two cups, one of which he took from her as he asked her to close her door.

"There is something you should know," he began, and then he told her what he knew, without going into every detail. He did however mention the meeting, the liaison that had continued for over a year, and the fact that she was now staying in a hotel in the city centre, not too far away from the office.

She sat listening, not wishing to believe anything she was hearing.

"Please keep this information confidential" he implored, "at least for a few days until things sort themselves out." Even to his ears, this reasoning sounded rather lame.

"Listen," he told her, "this may only be a flying visit and then she will return home again." He knew that this would not be the case, but still it had to be said.

"I shall have to tell his wife," she told her.

"I understand, but let's give ourselves a few days and see what transpires."

She had to admit that he could be right.

If the situation had evolved to such an extent, surely he would be obliged to advise his wife. She would be shattered, of that there was no doubt. They may have had their differences, but she knew that this type of news had to come from her husband and certainly not from anyone else.

"I have to go now," the PR said. "I have a few reports to write. Let's have lunch together soon, on me," he added, smiling at her.

She laughed and was happy that he had confided in her. There was certainly going to be a stir within the next few days, of that she was sure.

She opened her office window; suddenly she needed a breath of fresh air. *Rather him than me*, she thought as her phone rang from the reception.

THE CONFRONTATION

She confronted him upon his arrival home that evening, after his business trip which had taken him away for nearly a week.

In some intuitive manner, he was not really surprised at her reaction. He had always known that she was intelligent and therefore should have been ready for her questions, but he was not prepared for her outburst. *Perhaps it is better this way,* he thought to himself, listening closely to her questions.

Finally, he told her almost everything, from beginning to end, as easily as he could without trying to hurt her. He was not completely at ease with himself, nor with the situation.

She sat on the lounge sofa, listening to his every word. She had known that something was amiss, but all of this? Was she hearing correctly? He was telling her some unimaginable story about having fallen in love with someone half his age and that he planned to leave her for this woman. Just what she had expected to hear, she was not sure; perhaps one-night flings, or a brief affair a few months back, even a small separation just to put things back into perspective, but not this. A divorce ? Was that the word he had actually used? She hesitated, listening closer. Yes, he had used the word "divorce."

Suddenly she found that she could not find any words to fight back, to answer him. She had heard his arguments: that she was not a Muslim, did not understand his religion or lifestyle, had not converted to Islam when they had married, and now he had found someone who understood him and his beliefs. What was he telling her?

She had married him, knowing that he was of the Islamic faith, but not once had he suggested that she convert. She thought now of Mama, who had warned her of marrying someone of such a different culture and religion. She had laughed at the time, but now she was not laughing. She felt like shouting out loud but knew that no screams would escape from her mouth.

Her mouth had dried up, parched of water like a plant in the desert struggling to survive, and so she panicked. He must have noticed, for in those few seconds he handed her a glass of water. She must have asked for one but could not remember doing so. Gently he handed her a glass filled with bubbly water, as though these bubbles could wash away her fears and doubts.

So, she thought, sipping the water and trying to regain her calm, *he is leaving me.*

The tears finally welled up in her blue eyes. He felt a moment of total horror; somehow, things were not going to plan. He had thought that she would take all this in her stride, perhaps even be happy with his decision. He now understood only too well that this was not going to be the case, and he hated himself for putting her through such misery. He took his share of the blame for the breakdown of their marriage, but somewhere, somehow, he thought she would have taken the other half. He had been so wrong. He felt slightly ashamed and lost confidence as though her tears had left him dried out, instead of watering his appetite to continue. She put down the glass, adding softly that she was exhausted and now planned to retire for the evening.

He nodded, not daring to add anything further. She would fight back, of that he was sure. He was glad that the children were not around that evening. He had finally given in to his daughter's plea to study fashion in the States, and he knew that his son was planning to apply to a British university to study English and history. He imagined that his son would wish to stay with his mother for his final year at school; however, that would be his son's choice and he would abide by that. Enough had been said for one evening, and the kids would be informed in due time. He knew that their reaction would be hostile; they both loved their mother very much.

For a moment, he regretted having brought up the subject that evening, but knew that he had little choice now. He had made plans for the future, plans that did not concern her. He slowly opened a bottle of juice, put on the television, and sat down to watch the news. He thought about calling the hotel but decided against it. Tonight he was not in the mood for talking anymore. He was tired and felt a great lassitude come over him. He tried to foresee the future; surely it would be brighter, and a fresh start was what he needed and wanted. His girlfriend understood him and his values, so why did he feel so lost?

He closed his eyes and began to pray. Tonight he so needed to find peace, inner peace. The weeks ahead would be a hard battle, of that he was sure. He fell asleep accepting the uncertainty with apprehension. For once, his prayers did not appease his soul.

THE DIVORCE

It had been a short, hard, and very bitter divorce. She was determined to ruin him financially and thus ordered her lawyers to aim as high as they could.

In a certain manner, she won, but the money gave her little satisfaction. If satisfaction there was, it was seeing her husband bruised and hurt as well as practically ruined financially.

Other than that, her life would continue. She still had the children. At least they were both over eighteen now, so there had been no hassle over parental rights and visits.

Her son had made it clear from the beginning that he intended to stay with her until his schooling was completed and he left for university. Their daughter was already away studying in the States, so in that respect, there were no arguments.

She thought that she may take a holiday. First, she had to find a new home for herself and her son. Then perhaps she would travel around Europe and see many of the capitals, visit various museums and exhibitions, do anything she pleased. It had been many years since she had made her own decisions, and now was the right time to commence.

A new beginning, she told herself. She began to like the idea, more and more.

First a new home, then a few weeks with Mama, and after, well, time would tell. She began to smile for the first time in a long time.

THE ANNOUNCEMENT

He had, as the saying goes, "married in haste" and was now "repenting at leisure."

Sitting at his desk in the office, he asked himself if he really wanted to go home. He thought about calling her to say that he had a last-minute meeting followed by a dinner; he knew that she would believe him. He had never imagined that things would have turned sour so rapidly.

They had both been so much in love when he had brought her to Europe. Meeting her on that business trip had been like a flash of lightning in his life. He had left his family for her, lost half of his fortune in the proceeds, but had accepted this fact. He had her and that was all he had wanted; at least that was what he had thought at the time. However, life does not always follow the path we wish, he sighed, and now life with her was becoming rather a strain if not to say a burden on him. He had been stupid and reckless and had ended up losing his family, something he now sadly regretted.

The wedding had been a fair success. His son had attended, but he had been bitterly disappointed when his daughter turned down the invitation. She knew how much her presence there at his side meant to him, but she had been adamant on the subject. She had chosen to ignore his feelings, preferring to shout and swear at him. He still remembered the scene; it was not one he wished to recall.

He knew only too well that he had hurt them all; he had simply fallen in love with someone else. People do it all the time, but to be fair, he did have two children who had not accepted the fact that their father had decided to remarry someone much younger. Many harsh words had been said, but his wife had told the children that it was something that they all had to except, and that life would continue for all of them. It would not be the same, but she had told them that changes are often a necessity in life. He had admired her dealing of the situation after the divorce. He knew that she had wanted to ruin him financially, but she had been good with the kids and never tried to turn them against him. He had done that himself, without anyone's assistance.

He also knew that his religion had been the cause of several clashes between them; this antagonism had grown over several years prior to his leaving. When he had first met his new wife, she had been so young, so inexperienced, and always eager to please him. He had accepted all of this without giving it a second thought, never taking the time to ponder over the fact that he could become slightly bored with all of this. Naturally, there had been a few hiccups when he had first brought her over on that infamous trip, nearly three years ago. Now he realised what a mistake he had made, but weren't mistakes meant to be made in order to shed light on the stark reality of life? She had stayed on at the hotel until moving into the apartment in the town centre. He had never expected his exwife to have heard of the affair prior to that evening when she had confronted him and he had told her the facts.

The divorce had come through quickly, and he had found himself single again. Without giving much thought to the matter, he had decided rather quickly, too quickly perhaps, to remarry. His first big mistake!

His new wife moved into the villa, another mistake, he had quickly realised. New paintwork and modern furniture could not erase the memories the house held within its walls.

There had also been the question of religion. She had been so happy to convert to Islam; perhaps he should have given her more time to reflect, but there again he had not, blinded by her adoration and willingness to please. So he had sent her to Islamic classes, and she had begun to read the Koran. He had also brought over an imam, a teacher of the Islamic faith, to stay with them for a while. She seemed to enjoy her religious classes and took them very seriously, perhaps a little too much. But he had not seen what was unravelling, although it had all happened in front of his own eyes. She was becoming obsessed with religion, and that was not what he had anticipated.

She begged him to buy her a prayer rug for her birthday and to explain some of the more intricate passages within the holy book, and he had done so. He had planned to take her away to the sunshine for a few days for her birthday, but she had turned down his offer. She had started changing even then, he thought with sadness, but to please her, he bought the carpet. There exist many types of praying carpets. They are all characterized by the prayer niche, or *mihrab,* which has an arch-shaped design at the end of the carpet. This design must point towards Mecca while the rug is being used for prayers.

He had chosen a carpet destined purely for praying, which explains the inclusion of the directional niche in the centre. She had loved it and had started praying with him in the evenings, but she did not join him in early morning prayer. Somehow this would have been an intrusion into his life, and he would not have liked that. He advised her not to become overzealous in her quest for her new-found religion, but rather to take thing gently, make some friends, and start going into town; he had bought her a little car to provide her with transport when she needed it.

He began to get the impression that she was isolating herself and relying on him for everything, something he did not like. He knew now that he had been overpossessive with his first wife, and he had planned not to make the same mistake again. He, who had been attracted to her in moment of weakness and who had proceeded to mould her into a model wife and converted Muslim, was now paying a very high price. She had taken to wearing a headscarf, something he did not appreciate. However, he resisted telling her. He knew that she would be hurt, and was this not what he had been searching for? Was this one of the reasons he had married her?

They had never discussed having a family. He had always assumed, perhaps a little selfishly, that since he had two grown children, she would not think that he would wish another child. He had been wrong; she had mentioned the word "baby" a year after their first wedding anniversary. He had looked across the table at her little face and wondered how he was going to tell her that children were not in the cards. But her sense of excitement had won him over that evening, and he never got around to saying what he felt deep down. A baby was the last thing he needed or wanted in his life right now. He was attempting to build up his business affairs once again. He had not minded his ex-wife walking away with a large chunk of his portfolio assets. He had also to make sacrifices of downsizing; something he did not like, but it had been necessary in order to continue making money.

His children also cost him a fair amount each month. He knew that their mother participated in paying for their clothes, their hobbies, not to mention holidays. He paid for his son's university fees, whilst his mother paid for his small flat near the university. He, however, paid for his daughter's lavish lifestyle plus the apartment he had bought for her in the States. This had not come cheap, but then he had chosen one of the most desirable areas in the city, thinking mainly of her well-being and safety.

He knew that she was still angry with him, but at least they spoke regularly on the phone and he got to see her for dinner on his trips across the pond. The ice was beginning to thaw; the wall of hostility had been brought down slowly, although she was still on her guard with him. There was still quite a stretch of road to go between them, but time was a great healer and he believed that time would improve their relationship. She never mentioned his new wife, not that he really expected her to; she avoided the subject at all costs.

His mind returned to that eventful evening, the one where she had made her announcement whilst they were dining out at a restaurant.

He had been telling her that she should start learning a new language or subscribe to painting classes, something she had thought about a few months earlier, but then she had interrupted him.

"No classes," she had said. "I have you and now there is going to be a baby."

"A baby?" he heard himself repeat her words.

"Yes, I just found out this morning, we are going to have a baby in October."

He sat there, not knowing what to say.

"Are you not happy?" she asked him.

"Yes, I am," he replied automatically. "It has just come as rather a shock to me."

"But are you really happy?" she asked him again.

It was then that he knew he was not. *Something is missing*, he heard himself think, but he knew that he was talking to his soul and to nobody else.

He had suddenly needed to get out of the restaurant; he knew that he had hurt her, he had read it all over her face. For a moment he hated himself and felt an overwhelming amount of guilt.

He missed his wife at this moment and his children; he missed their laughter, even the shouting matches, but above all his wife's blue eyes. His phone rang in his office, and he was suddenly brought back to that afternoon.

It was the receptionist, telling him that his chauffeur was ready.

"Thanks," he answered. "Please tell him that I shall be down in five minutes."

He unlocked the bottom drawer of his desk and brought out a picture in a silver frame. It had been lying there for three years now. He looked at it carefully before placing it back in the drawer, which he then locked before picking up his briefcase and making his way to the elevator. *Yes, we all make mistakes in life,* he thought, but his mistake was a difficult one to rectify, almost impossible.

A Chance Meeting

Due to Air Traffic Control (ATC), the airport was chaotic. Airlines have the hard task of either cancelling or consolidating flights.

She was returning home after a two-week stay with Mama, who had just celebrated her seventy-eighth birthday. She had been delighted to see her daughter and naturally had bombarded her with questions regarding her grandchildren: How were they doing? Was her granddaughter happy in the States, and how about that fine grandson, was he enjoying life at university?

Mama had understood very quickly how hurt her daughter had been a few years back and tried to avoid any questions relating to her exhusband. She neither criticised the situation nor said, "I told you so"; no, this would not have been correct, and she loved her daughter too much to make such comments.

She did, however, notice that her daughter had learned quickly to stand on her own feet, and the past couple of years, in a way, had been good for her. She had travelled and made sure the children were happy and continuing their studies; she even had the occasional date, but nothing ever seemed to come out of these meetings. She was still strikingly beautiful; fortunately, her mother thought, the hurt had never turned into bitterness. She had inner peace now which only made her look more radiant. She had been very angry at the way in which her daughter had been treated; *what mother would not be?* she often thought. She had always suspected that their differences in culture would one day turn against them, and unfortunately, much to her regret, she had been right, a fact she had kept to herself.

They hugged and said their good-byes; she had ordered a taxi to take her daughter to the airport. The weather had been very poor recently, with bad visibility, but she hoped that the flight would not be delayed too much. She knew how anxious her daughter was to get back. Her son was arriving home the following afternoon, and she knew how important that was to her.

In the taxi, her daughter thought that perhaps there could be some serious delays due to the bad weather; having been in the airline business, she knew quite a bit about airline scheduling. However, when she got to the airport, she saw the flight was scheduled for departure with only a possible delay, so as she boarded, she was confident that all would be well.

Just before take-off, the pilot's voice announced that the flight would be delayed for up to thirty minutes. "This is due to ATC; we apologise to all our passengers for any inconvenience this may cause."

True to his words, they were airborne twenty-five minutes later, and she kept her fingers crossed that she would still be able to make her connecting flight. The plane touched down an hour later, approximately thirty minutes later than scheduled. They had been unable to catch up on any lost time during the flight, due to heavy head winds. The first thing she did after leaving the aircraft was to pass security, then she made her way into the departure hall in order to find her flight gate on the screen. It showed that flight number 732 was now boarding, and she made her way quickly to the gate, only stopping for a brief moment to buy a magazine. Her high heels could be heard echoing against the airport flooring.

She made the flight, just in time. She noticed as she walked into the cabin that all the other passengers were already seated, luggage stored, and were now either chatting or flicking through the day's newspapers. She was shown to her seat, where she quickly stored her handbag under the seat in front of her, with a sigh of relief. She noticed that the seat next to the window was vacant and was quite happy not to have to chat to anyone. She just wanted to be alone with her thoughts.

Just then, she heard an announcement from the captain. Their take-off slot had been delayed by twenty minutes, which would allow a last-minute passenger to board; they would then close up and go. She took out her magazine and began to glance through the pages, the majority being advertisements for perfume, lipsticks, bags, and shoes. *There are more ads than articles*, she thought, wondering why she had stopped to buy it. It was at this precise moment that she looked up from her reading and caught a glimpse of the delayed passenger. She could not believe her eyes: it was him, her exhusband, who was now being shown to his seat, front row aisle. He had always chosen that seat, she remembered, when travelling on commercial airlines. *Old habits die hard*, she thought to herself, smiling.

Her heart began to beat so loudly that she was under the impression that the other passengers would hear it; her throat dried up. She tried to call out to him, to say hello, but no words adventured out. She had not seen him since their divorce, although she had often thought about him.

Had he seen her? She did not think he had, as there had been no eye contact. Suddenly they were told to ensure that all seat belts were fastened, as take-off was imminent. The plane began to taxi out onto the runway.

Once they had been airborne for around fifteen minutes, the crew commenced serving drinks and refreshments. She watched her exhusband closely. He was reading the *Times* magazine and hardly glanced at the hostess, as she offered him a choice of drinks. Soon it was her turn to be served—she suddenly had an idea; could she possibly carry it out? She requested a small bottle of champagne and then, as if on second thought, asked for a second one.

"Could I also have two glasses?" she asked the hostess.

Taking a deep breath and waiting for the drinks trolley to pass up the aisle, she slowly got up from her seat and proceeded to walk down to the front row. She stood still for a moment before tapping him on the shoulder. He looked up.

"What a surprise!" he said. "Where did you come from?"

"Two rows behind," she said, smiling and swallowing hard before continuing, "There's a spare seat next to me, would you care to join me?"

He hesitated and she regretted her flippant remark. He was, she feared, going to decline her invitation.

"I think that would be rather nice," he answered quietly.

They took their seats; she sat in the window seat, allowing him the comfort of the aisle.

"So, how are you?" he asked her politely.

"Fine, I am just returning from two weeks with Mama."

"Is she keeping well?" he inquired gently

"Oh just great, you know Mama; we were celebrating her birthday, and you know how she loves these things."

He looked at her and then at the champagne bottles.

"I see that you are planning a celebration, am I right?"

"Not really," she said, blushing. "I just felt like enjoying a glass of bubbly. I couldn't tempt you to join me, could I?"

It had not gone unnoticed to his trained eye that there were two glasses sitting on the small pull-down table. "Perhaps you were expecting company?" he asked her.

She blushed again, and he noticed that she was at a loss as to what to answer. He saw her flush and thought how lovely she looked.

"So, how is life treating you?" she asked him, desperate to find some composure.

"Why don't I pour you a drink first?" he said, and then he stopped. The sight of her had given him a much bigger jolt than he could have ever expected; if he was to be honest, he suddenly felt a lot happier than he had in months.

He found himself pouring a little champagne into the second glass wondering what on earth he was doing. *This was an act of weakness on his part, not to mention going against all his beliefs,* this much he knew, but on the spur of that precise moment he did not know how to stop himself.

"Mind if I join you?" he said, without any warning,

"No, I would love you to"

She turned and looked at him as they raised their glasses. Their eyes met and held, just for that second too long.

"I have missed you," he said.

"Really?" she replied, lowering her eyes.

"But I think that you knew that."

"Should I?" she said, almost inaudibly. "The children tell me that you are about to become a father again."

He did not answer her immediately. "I do not think that this is the time or place to discuss that matter," he said.

She remained silent for loss of words. She should not have brought up the question about the baby.

He obviously did not wish to tell her about his new life. In fact, she should never have gone over to speak to him at all; what had she been thinking about? They were divorced, had not seen each other in several years, and here she was acting like some stupid sixteen-year-old. *At least the flight is not a long one,* she thought, *and soon we shall be landing and he will disappear out of my life again.*

She heard him say, "How about meeting up for dinner sometime next week?"

What to say, she did not know. Where would this lead, to more heartache? It was then that she saw he had sipped his champagne. It had been many years since she had seen him do such a thing, ceasing all alcohol and requesting her to do likewise. He too was thinking, as the taste of the champagne took him back when life had been fun and they had been so much in love. Hadn't things been better then, without all his religious principles, principles he had requested her to follow also? The thought sobered him.

She studied him closely and noticed that he was deep in thought. *I don't believe he is totally happy*, she thought.

"Yes," she finally said. "I think that I can manage dinner next week."

"Good, then let's finish our drinks before we are asked to fasten up for touchdown."

THE LOBBYIST, PART 2

He had waited a couple of days before phoning his travelling companion. He took out the business card he had been handed on the plane and read it again: "Chairman," and the name of an investment company he had never heard of.

If the truth be known, he was curious about this man and wanted to find out a little more about him; in fact, he wanted to know who he was. As always, he wondered if there would be something in it for him. He was always keen for a financial gain, and so perhaps that was the reason he made the call.

The mobile number was answered quickly, and he recognised the voice at the other end of the line as being the one he had spoken to on the plane; an unusual intonation. Good English, he thought, but certainly not his mother tongue. He had no idea where he had been born, but he was obviously not of European descent; Middle East, perhaps?

"Thanks for calling me," the voice answered, bringing him back to life.

"No problem," he replied. "How are you?"

"Fine, when can we meet?"

Slightly taken aback by his abruptness, he quickly said, "How about later this afternoon?"

"Perfect, we can meet around five o'clock and, perhaps after our discussion, have a light dinner. If you have the time?"

"Sure, sounds fine to me. I look forward to seeing you later."

As he put down the phone, the lobbyist thought that he was still no wiser as to their forthcoming meeting; what were they going to discuss? *Should be interesting, though*, he thought to himself, making his way to the hotel bar, where he ordered a bloody Mary. A bit too early in the day to start drinking, but alcohol always relaxed him when he had something on his mind. Perhaps this was an excuse he gave himself, as he knew that his consumption of spirits had risen these last few months. *Not to worry, I can give it up whenever I want, or can I?* He thought upon reflection. He suddenly remembered that the guy had only drunk mineral water throughout the entire flight. *Oh my God, I hope he is not a non-drinker*, he thought, hoping that they may indulge in a good bottle of Bourgogne wine that evening over dinner. He preferred not to drink alone when dining, but then he could make an exception if this guy had anything really interesting to talk over. He ordered another drink before making his way up to his room, a large double with a view overlooking the lake. He showered and changed his shirt. He put on a new tie, nothing too bright, combed his hair, and looked in the mirror, liking what he saw.

He had noted on his pad that he must remember to give a call to that young lady he had met last week in the French bistro. He had been rather stricken with her, something that rarely happened to him. *Perhaps she is the type of person I could eventually settle down with*, he thought. She had been so different from the other women he dated. She was pretty but possessed an intelligence and warmth also, three things that did not necessarily go together. *However*, he thought, *now is hardly the time to be thinking of my personal life*. He would definitely give her a call later on this evening, when he returned to the hotel after his meeting and dinner, time difference being on his side.

He arrived at the offices just after 16.35. *Fine*, he thought, *now let us see what he has to offer.*

He paid the taxi and stepped out into the warm sunshine. The car had dropped him off in front of the offices, and he quickly ran up the three steps and into the reception area. Here he was greeted by a young Asian; *security, no doubt*, he thought. He gave his name and handed over one of his business cards, stating that he had an appointment with the chairman. The guard then made a phone call, and he was informed that someone would be down to meet him shortly.

He noticed that there was a receptionist sitting behind a rather large desk adorned with a bouquet of white roses. She seemed to be rather busy, although she finally took the time to come over and explained that the chairman's personal assistant was on her way down and would take him upstairs to the seventh floor.

For a moment, he wondered why she could not have taken him herself, but then a phone rang and he saw that she was also the office telephonist. And so he waited.

True to her word, the glass elevator opened and out stepped a very attractive blonde; *well*, he thought, *all is not lost*.

The lady in question was a cool number, of that there was no doubt. She was dressed in a black leather skirt, not too short but just the length to show off a great pair of legs. She wore a tight fitting black jacket, under which she wore an ivory-coloured silk top. She wore no jewellery other than a small pair of diamond earrings. He liked what he saw. As she put forth her slender hand to introduce herself, he noticed the glittering of a white diamond wedding ring, complete with an emerald-and-diamond engagement ring. *A real class act the guy has here*, he thought while they went up in the lift. Once in the elevator, they both exchanged cordial pleasantries, and he had the time to see that her sparkling eyes matched the colour of her ring.

Well, whatever his business is, he certainly knows how to pick them, he thought. *He obviously can afford the best.* This thought was jolted as the lift stopped and she led him down a hallway.

The floor he saw was entirely in wood panelling, with a number of doors leading off the corridor. She knocked on one of the doors and entered without waiting for an answer.

He walked into a very large office, and there behind a desk was his travelling companion.

However, today he was immaculately dressed, wearing a grey suit with a slight sheen to it. To complete the outfit, he wore a white shirt and what appeared to be an Italian silk tie in a shade of Bordeaux. *So*, he thought, *here is the chairman.*

They shook hands warmly, and the lobbyist took it upon himself to remark how lovely the offices were.

"Glad you like it," the chairman answered. "And I see that you have already met my PA."

He almost answered flippantly, "I sure have," but thought the better of it and, instead, replied in an even, polite tone that he had been delighted to meet such a lovely person.

"Would you care for some tea or coffee?" the PA asked him.

He turned round to look at her once again before replying, "No thanks, I am just fine," without adding that a drink might have been more than welcome.

She then quietly left the office and disappeared through another door.

The chairman invited him to sit down, and he took a chair opposite the chairman's desk and waited for him to continue.

"Well, I guess you are wondering why I asked you here this afternoon."

"I want to propose a business deal, but first let me explain further," the man sitting opposite him said.

He wondered for a fleeting moment what was coming next.

"I have the money and you may have the honey."

He almost laughed out loud. This phrase sounded like some folksong lyric he had heard, but he could not remember who sang it.

"You told me that you are interested in the world of lobbying, and I have interest in hiring a lobbyist to assist me with a future project I have in mind. Interested?"

"Continue," was all he replied, wishing to know a little more about the project, but perhaps his coming here this afternoon was going to turn out worthwhile. Lobbying is synonymous with money and ambition, so maybe there would be something in it for him.

The chairman continued, "I know that your country has been recently plagued with climate catastrophes, particularly in the South. I have drawn up a contingency plan to help out this deprived area and build it up into something really strong, for the people living there, the environment, and the economic development of the area. However, in order to proceed with this, I require assistance. You mentioned on the plane that you are a lawyer and involved on occasions with lobbying. Is that correct?"

"I certainly am," he replied, "and I think that I may be able to assist you on this, once I know which area you are talking about. My father is a well-known senator, and I shall certainly get in touch with him, but first I would like to hear some more about this project you have in mind."

"I'm delighted that you are interested," his host replied.

"To be honest, I have various ideas I would like to put forth to you and would be interested in having your thoughts on the matter. I wish to invest in your part of the world and know very well that if I am to get anywhere with my plans, money is not enough. I need to be introduced to the right people, know the legislations of the city, and become known to the people that can make things move. Do I make myself clear?"

"So," the lobbyist answered him, "you are looking for someone such as my good self to get you introduced, do I follow you correctly?"

"Exactly," the chairman said. "I need someone who has access to the right people, who can introduce me and my team to the contacts who will eventually assist in pushing through some of my ideas. This is a priority. And after all, when all is said and done, there are always those who have the final say. Are you interested so far?"

"I am indeed, and I think that I can be of help to you, but let me think things over, talk it over with some friends on the phone, and we can resume discussions over dinner."

"Fine," the chairman said. "How about meeting up at LaMasena, say around 19.30?"

"Sounds great to me," he answered.

"Now if you'd like, my chauffeur and I will drop you off at your hotel; it's on our way, and I am sure that you wish some time to relax. When are you planning to return home?"

"In a couple of days."

"Good," he said, lifting the phone to ring his PA and advise her that he was now leaving for the remainder of the day.

She came back in to the office to say good-bye to them both.

"Let's hope that we shall meet again," the lobbyist told her.

"Yes," she answered, "I shall look forward to your next visit.

The pair of them left the office, taking the lift down to the reception area, where the chauffeur was awaiting them. He saw that the car was a Rolls Royce, the colour of midnight blue. The interior was entirely fitted in a light caramel colour, a rather unusual colour, the lobbyist thought, but then it was surely custom made. The guy obviously had bucks, and lots of them.

They drove along the lake road, and after crossing one the main bridges in the city, they soon arrived at his hotel. The lobbyist got out, thanking the chauffeur, and confirmed the time of their meeting that evening, after which he made his way into the hotel lobby.

As he walked to the reception area to collect his room key, he thought to himself that his afternoon had been quite a surprise. He had expected the initial meeting to continue longer, but that it had finished quickly actually suited him much better. This short interlude gave him the time to place a call through to his father and get a feeling on the tenders already out on this one. He knew exactly what he had been talking about and was interested in hearing his plans to develop the deprived area. Also, he wanted to make another important call, one to a certain young lady, asking her to keep Friday evening free. He hoped to be home by then, and he planned on getting to know her a lot better over the forthcoming weekend.

The first call to his father had provided him with important information that he knew would be useful, and his second call, much to his delight, was also positive. *So this trip is going well,* he thought to himself, taking a small drink out of his mini bar. *Celebrations are in order,* he thought, smiling.

He arrived first at the restaurant and ordered double vodka on ice at the bar. After having spoken to his father, he was now anxious to learn just how much money the chairman had to invest and what exactly he planned to do with the money. Money talks, that was a well-known adage, but he had to tread carefully. He did not wish to appear overly keen or promise something he could not carry out. His lawyer instincts always kept him pretty close to reality when negotiating a lobbying contract, something he was glad about. Lobbying was a serious matter, one that should always be handled with care.

The chairman arrived five minutes later, and they were shown to their reserved table. It was set in a booth style which gave them plenty of opportunity for private and discreet discussions. The waiter asked them if they cared for a drink prior to ordering.

"A vodka tonic for me," the lobbyist said.

"And a mineral water will be just fine," his companion added.

So his guess had been correct, the chairman did not drink alcohol.

Oh, to hell with it, he thought; he would do the drinking and the listening and his new friend could do the talking.

The menu was brought and they both chose a mixed salad for starters and a Chateaubriand for two.

He was then asked if he would care for some wine with his meal.

"I would, actually," the lobbyist said, "but please go ahead and choose. I hope that you will join me." He added this phrase to ensure that his assumption had been right.

"I do not drink alcohol," his dining companion answered, "but please be my guest and enjoy whatever you would like."

He chose a bottle of Chevrey Chambertin1986, one of his favourite Bourgognes, and was only sorry that he would have to drink it alone. He did not think it wise to bring up the question of alcohol, but he did not have to wait long before his unasked question was answered.

"I am a Muslim," the chairman said, "which is why I do not drink any type of alcohol."

Oh my God, he thought to himself, *a Muslim; why did I not work that one out before? This could make things a bit tricky concerning contacts within his country. These were the guys who had blown up the Twin Towers several years ago. Might not be an easy sales pitch back in the States. However, the guy seems pretty genuine, and he doesn't want to drink, so be it. That's his problem, not mine, and as I am here, we might as well get to the bottom of this idea.*

What he actually answered was, "That's fine by me, but thank you, I shall take full advantage of your kind hospitality."

The chairman laughed and said that would be no problem. "I have my own principles that I live by," he told the lobbyist, "and you have yours. End of story."

The lobbyist relaxed, liking his straightforward attitude. The previous vodka had worked wonders, especially the double he had downed upon his arrival. This helped him now settle down to enjoy the evening.

"Now tell me more about your project," he said.

"It's like this: I have a considerable amount of money to invest; the exact figure, I prefer not to mention at this point in time. I would like this money to work for me, while at the same time doing some good in today's world.

"My idea would be to build a new town, a town in the same place as the one that had been recently devastated. I want to build several large hotels, casinos, and eventually an air strip. In this way, we can entice wealthy individuals to visit the town, either in the hotels for business venues or in the casinos, where they can spend their money. This would bring work to the town and assist in building new homes for the homeless, whilst at the same time offering them the chance to build my vision of a completely new and green area. It promotes employment to an impoverished area and reconstructs an entire city. Priority, obviously, has to be given to the building of small homes for the locals, to enable them to be sheltered before commencing on the project.

"The hotels will be five star, and I plan to bring in the best interior designers around; hopefully, within years, this town will be reborn.

"What do you think about the project so far?" he asked the lobbyist.

"Do you have schematics I can look over?"

"I do, but they have to be enlarged still; some of my staff are working out additional details as we speak. Give me a week or two and I shall have them sent to you by courier service."

The lobbyist studied the man sitting opposite him. He spoke well, he certainly had an idea in his head, and actually what he was proposing was immense, but he had to admit it could be possible.

He knew the area in question had been almost wiped out with the last hurricane, and help like this was desperately needed. He knew from his discussion with his father earlier that day that several suggestions for rebuilding the city had been put forward and that tenders were already in the pipeline, but this was a completely new concept and was so incredible that it might just work. He felt the adrenaline in his body beginning to flow.

"You proposal sounds very interesting," he told his friend. "Naturally, we have to go over the logistics of such a programme very carefully, but I think that I may be just the man to get you get the right contacts. Have you spoken with anybody else outside of your office regarding this project?"

"No, the idea is still being worked out and, of course, needs to be finalized; many of the plans are still at the drawing-board level. After meeting you on the plane, I decided you were the man to talk things over with, at least initially."

"Good," the lobbyist replied. "I promise nothing but will definitely discuss this matter with friends when I return home. I will give you a ring next week. You must understand that for this type of work, time is essential. I shall await your schematics but have to tell you that it will be quite some time before you get a final answer. First, you and I have to draw up a binding contract outlining the fact that you have requested me to do some lobbying on your behalf. This is essential in order to keep matters correct. We can decide on the financial aspect of my consulting fees the next time you are over. I shall start some groundwork prior to any contract being signed, and we will take things from there. How does this sound to you?"

"I understand very clearly and am prepared to pay you good money for assisting me; however, let's enjoy our dinner now and we can discuss things further once you have some solid material in hand."

The food and wine were excellent, and the lobbyist soon found himself enjoying his evening and, surprisingly enough, the company. The chairman was interesting to talk to and had a sound knowledge of business ethics, something he would not have thought on a first impression.

They looked at the dessert menu and he picked tiramisu.

"Good choice," his friend told him. "An all time favourite of mine."

From that moment on, they had become friends; it was an unlikely friendship, but one that would last a long time. The bond was forged that evening, quickly but truly. To be honest, the lobbyist was not given to feeling any empathy towards his clients, but the chairman seemed a genuine type; with all his obvious wealth, he remained simple and discreet, possessing none of the aggressiveness or arrogance he often saw in his brash, harsh world of money. Often people with wealth thought that they could buy anything and anyone, but he seemed to have none of those traits.

No, the chairman spoke about his family with a great deal of love and affection. He learned that evening he had two children he obviously adored and a wife to whom he had been married for over twenty years. *Hopefully*, he thought, *I can get something going for his project*. It may not be the easiest task he had been asked to perform, but it was one that, in a favourable light, could be highly beneficial to both of them.

On his next trip, he had been invited to his friend's home, a stunning villa on the lakeshore. Once again he admired the surroundings and the beautiful and tastefully furnished home. He met his lovely wife and was introduced to his two teenage children. Some may say that he had it all: a wonderful family, anything money could buy, and a religion he followed without question. Surely he could never have any doubts or wonder sometimes if he had made the right decision. He was essentially a man of all seasons, he thought.

He understood that his friend was a deeply religious man, or at least one who followed his faith without questions. Deep down, he admired this; his family was not a particularly religious one. Sure, they went to church at Christmas and knew the Easter hymns, but perhaps there was something missing. For the first time in a long time, he began to wonder about himself and his own lifestyle. Surely there was something lacking behind all the bravado and facade that he put on and accepted in others so readily. He knew his friend's wife was not a Muslim; she had not converted to this religion, something his friend had told him. She appeared to live in that huge house alone with their many servants. One occasion, he had invited them both out for dinner and had noticed that she did not drink either. At their home, there had been no show of any type of alcohol, and he had not been offered anything other than water or fruit juice. He accepted this fact without too much question, but it had crossed his mind later that perhaps his friend inflicted this on his wife rather than her choosing this path. It was, after all, nothing to do with him, and he thought no more about it.

However, a crack showed up a number of months later. His friend was over for a business meeting pertaining to his project, and he had invited a few friends and business associates, including his father, to a meeting. The schematics had been sent over as promised, and he had been able to gather quite a number of interested parties willing to invest in such a venture. It looked as though things could begin to take shape.

It had been after this fruitful meeting that his friend had told him that he and his wife were separating. He took the news calmly, not wishing to make any comment other than, "I'm sorry to hear that."

But he wondered what had engineered this changing of heart. They had seemed such a happy family. It was only the next evening over dinner that his friend took him into his confidence, telling him that he met someone else, a young girl, almost twenty years younger. They had met by chance at a dinner party and had ultimately fallen in love, something the lobbyist found rather difficult to believe, coming from someone he had grown to like and trust. Sex was one thing, but he doubted that his friend could have fallen so much in love so quickly with God knows what girl; this, he seriously doubted.

However, he later had to admit, he had been proven wrong in his thinking.

Several months later, there had been a rather difficult and highly expensive divorce, followed by a rather hasty marriage. He had been invited to the wedding, and due to his heavy commitment to the forthcoming project and taking into consideration their friendship, he and his girlfriend both attended. It had been a simple affair, with very few guests, mainly his family. He remembered his son, who had been present and who had looked rather uncomfortable in the strange surroundings. It had been very hot and humid that day which had not assisted in the rather bizarre wedding celebrations.

This perhaps not being the correct adjective, he thought later, but at the time it had seemed this way.

He had assumed, once again wrongly, that she must be pregnant, hence the quick wedding. He could not imagine his friend wishing any newborn baby to arrive out of wedlock. But no, she had not been pregnant, at least not at that time. He had learned prior to the wedding that the young lady in question was taking lessons, thus enabling her to convert to Islam prior to the wedding; his friend had explained to him on the phone that the forthcoming wedding was to be a union of love and mutual spiritual minds. This was not exactly his mode of speech when describing the reason for marrying. He was on the verge of getting engaged to the young lady he had met that night in the bistro, but he was happy to say that their wedding would not be a spiritually based one.

However, each man must lead the life he chooses, he thought. If the guy was happy, then who was he to criticise him or to raise questions? He would leave that to his friend's wife and family, both of whom he knew had been extremely perturbed at the arrival of this young lady into his life, not to mention the subsequent events, leading up to a hostile divorce and a rather hasty marriage.

A year after the wedding, business was going well for his friend, and it looked as though his life was now set out like a road map, one of peace and harmony. They had attended his own wedding a few months after their own, and he had to admit that although she was young and rather shy, she appeared to be very much in love with her new husband. *Maybe I got it all wrong*, he had thought much later. He had not had a lot of time to spend with them, as theirs had been a large society wedding with many of his father's friends as well as his own business associates present.

It was the phone call that worried him. He had called his friend to advise him that his tender on the hotels had been accepted and that work on the constructing site should start within the next few months. He wanted to know when he was planning his next visit in order to get the architects and engineers together for a sit-down meeting, in order to thrash out any last-minute details that may have been overlooked. He heard straight away from his friend's voice that all was not well. He sounded tired and listless, and he was not really interested in what he was telling him. He asked if everything was well but was told not to worry and was assured that everything was in order. He had hung up, but with quite a number of doubts in his mind.

He was flying to Europe the following week and decided to make a detour to see his friend and find out just what was going on. It was then that he was convinced everything was all but well. His friend had not opened up to him, much to his regret, but rather spoke of a new baby on the way. He somehow seemed preoccupied about the affair, although to be fair he did not actually say as much. He had only heard the previous week that his own wife was expecting, and so he had hoped to celebrate the good news with his friend. However, he had not brought up the subject of his own wife's new pregnancy, doubting that the subject was not one on which to dwell.

His friend only brightened up that evening at dinner when he also told him about having met his exwife unexpectedly on board a recent flight from the United Kingdom. He knew, of course, that their son was studying in a university over there and thought it not too strange that they had perhaps met up on a visit. However, it appeared that this had not been the case and that this chance meeting had rather made his friend blow caution to the wind. Not in his nature, the lobbyist thought. Could it possibly be that it had come to flesh over faith? Knowing this man as he now did, he knew that this would cause turmoil in his mind. His religion and faith meant so much to him. Did he now doubt his choice? Was this the reason for his tormented look, the weariness in his speech? He, who had always been so sure and decisive in all his undertakings, could it be possible that he was now having doubts or, worse still, regrets? He looked lost, like a man at a crossroads not knowing which road to take and, worse still, not daring to think what would happen if he took the wrong one. *If only he would tell me a bit more,* the lobbyist thought. The sadness in his eyes was unbearable to watch; if only he had pushed further, forced his friend to confide in him, then perhaps things could have worked out differently.

He hated leaving him in this way; however, outside the hotel, his friend had warmly embraced him and said, "I'll be just fine. I have a few things on my mind. Forgive me if I was not good company this evening, it is just that I have to sort out some personal matters, nothing important, so please don't worry, my dear friend. Give my regards to your lovely wife, and we shall be in touch soon."

They bade each other farewell, promising to speak soon on the phone.

"Bon voyage" was the last thing his friend had called out before getting into his car.

The lobbyist could never have anticipated what would transpire over the following months.

THE BIRTH OF A BABY GIRL

The baby was born when he was away from home, travelling on a business trip.

She had sat down to watch a film when her waters broke; she panicked at first and then called the security guard outside the villa. He in turn calmly called an ambulance before making his way up to the house. He was surprised that his boss had left his wife alone with the birth of the baby so near, but then nothing he did these days seemed to add up. Endless business trips, a number of evening engagements, something he found strange; neither of them normally went out in the evenings, and in particular the chairman, and on his own. But recently he had taken to going out a fair amount during the week, leaving his heavily pregnant wife alone in the house. It was totally out of character with the man he had known for several years, and he hoped that the forthcoming birth would not be too difficult.

The ambulance men soon arrived and, seeing the situation, decided to take her straight into hospital, as the birth appeared imminent. They had been informed that it was her first baby and therefore decided that no chances should be taken. And so she found herself giving birth in a sterile room, surrounded by hospital staff she did not know, and only the guard waiting outside in the corridor for comfort, if comfort was the right word. She did not mind the pain that was being inflicted upon her; if only he had been here at her side, things would be just perfect. She had so planned this event, her husband sitting and holding her hand while she gave birth to their baby. But things had not turned out the way she had hoped. He had been so preoccupied frequently, surely with business matters, items he never discussed with her. However, he had also been a little distant, but as she cried out yet again, she ceased to think about anything other than giving birth. She gave one more push as requested, and the baby arrived. The doctor placed the baby on her stomach before cutting the umbilical cord. *She is beautiful,* she thought, looking down at the baby. *Why could he not have been here for those precious moments?*

As tiredness came over her, the baby was taken away, and she was left to rest after having been sponged down and her gown changed. She soon fell asleep.

The next morning, she was moved to a private room. The guard had come to see her and told her that they had waited to ensure all was well before calling her husband with the good news. What, in fact, they decided to do was call the PR manager and advise him that she was in labour. He had requested that they let him know the moment the baby arrived; in this manner, he would announce the good news to the boss.

He gave him the news as soon as possible and congratulated him on the new arrival.

"Just let me call the clinic and speak to my wife, and then we shall think about returning home," he had told him.

She lifted the phone and knew that it had to be him.

"Hi," he said, "so we have a baby daughter?"

"She is just beautiful," his wife announced. "Just wait till you see her. She has your eyes, you know."

"I'll be flying back as soon as possible. Make sure that you get plenty of rest; you will need all your strength soon."

He then went out and phoned his PA with the good news.

"Can you order a large bouquet of flowers to send on my behalf?" he asked her.

"Sure," she said after congratulating him. "Any particular message you would like on the card?"

"No," he replied, "just make out something nice."

The PA was slightly taken aback. She had planned to send an arrangement of flowers from the office but had assumed that her boss would send his own message. After all, it was his baby; to her way of reasoning, surely the message should come from his heart. However, she would write a few lines.

Upon arriving at the hospital the following evening, he saw the flowers and knew at once that his PA had done an excellent job, as always. He liked and trusted her, and hoped that she knew this.

For Muslims, as well as for Christians, a new baby is a great time for rejoicing.

When he saw his wife and the baby girl, she told him, "A baby is like a favour from Allah."

He knew that she was correct but even he was a little taken aback at her first words to him.

Normally, when a baby is born into the Muslim faith, someone (normally the father) leans over the right ear of the baby and pronounces the word "*L'adhan*" (a call for prayer). In the left ear, "*L'iqamah*" is also recited, announcing the beginning of prayer. He knew that this was what she expected, so when the baby had been brought to him, he did exactly that, knowing that this ritual should have been carried out right after the birth and not a day later. However, he was happy to offer his little girl his prayers and felt a slight pang of guilt at not having been present for the birth. The baby was now almost two days old, and he knew that they had seven days before naming her. If this was the ritual his wife wanted, then so be it.

He suddenly felt tired for no apparent reason, perhaps not tired, but early. How long could his life continue in this manner? *Now there is the baby to think of,* he told himself. *I shall have to make my decision sooner than later.* He would have given anything to be elsewhere right at this moment but knew that this was impossible, even to him. The meeting with his exwife had troubled him far more than he could have thought possible. He could not get her out of his head and knew that he had to see her again soon, very soon. He had never realised just how much he had missed her until seeing her in front of him.

Looking up, he saw that his wife was speaking to him; not understanding what she had said, he asked her to repeat her comment.

"I am so happy now," she told him.

The following silence was totally unbearable to both of them.

"Yes, of course you are; I am too," he told her. "How could I not be?"

So now he was lying not only to himself but to his wife. He suddenly took her hand in his as if this gesture could wipe out all other thoughts.

Sadly, this was not to be.

THE DINNER DATE

He had thought many times of their meeting up. A chance encounter, but an encounter he found very difficult to erase from his mind.

Seeing his ex-wife again after these few years had been incredible, something he wasn't ready for, neither the impact she had had on him. He had wanted to reach out and touch her when she had been sitting next to him on the plane, something he knew was totally impossible. She had looked so desirable and yet a little vulnerable, so much so, that his feelings scared him, perhaps for the first time in his life. He, who prided himself in always being in control of every situation, business or pleasure, had been like putty in her hands. He had invited her for dinner on the spur of the moment, or had it really been that, he wondered. He wanted to see her again, maybe even more. She had appeared totally at ease with him, but then it had been a short flight, and she could have been putting a face on things.

He wanted to call her, but more so he knew he wanted her back in his life, and this was not altogether a dinner date. He tried to talk himself out of calling her but knew that eventually he would. However, there was his new wife, not to mention the baby to consider. Yes, he loved the baby, but his wife was now a completely different person from the one he had married. She had become someone else, and this new identity did not please him. To be fair, she had done nothing wrong; it was just her dedication to Islam, her manner of dressing nowadays. He had loved her once, she had been there for him when he felt the need for someone, and he had fallen in love. The poor girl was still in her twenties, and he was already bored. Now the excitement was over, the roles had changed, perhaps he had let things go too far and he worried that now was rather late for such thoughts. To a certain extent, he had moulded her into the person she now was. He knew this to be a fact. She had followed his beliefs blindly, believing in his love, and he knew that somewhere, somehow, he had let her down. He could see no way out. He wanted to be free again, but how?

She was wonderful with the baby, this he had to admit. It was not that he had been left out in the cold. She included him in everything concerning their daughter and had tried to make him love her again, as before. He knew that it would not be long before she began to suspect that something was wrong. He had never thought of leaving her, that is, not until the chance meeting with his ex-wife. Now he found that he wanted some excitement and joy back in his life, and she was the person that could bring him this happiness. Why did she have this knock-out effect on him? He had left her for better things, his principles, and now all he wanted was to have her back.

He read the mail and then went to pick up the phone but decided better. *No, I shall wait till tomorrow*, he thought, *otherwise she may think that I am running after her again.* Instead, he called in his PA and asked her to go through the mail with him, saying that he wished to dictate some letters.

By tomorrow, I shall be a lot calmer, he thought, *and will see matters in a different light.*

He could not have known that his ex-wife was also thinking of their meeting in the plane; she recalled that he had promised to ring her concerning a possible dinner date. She was pretty sure that he would call; she felt that he had changed somehow but could not quite work out how. Had he really said that he missed her? She had not dared say how much she had missed him. She had gone through what is known as a love-hate relationship ever since the divorce, one day hating him, and the next longing for his return. It had all seemed so impossible until their meeting by chance on the plane the other afternoon. She knew how his life was going; she heard from the children, mainly her son, and knew also that he sometimes asked after her. She was surprised when she heard the news about the baby, but then it was inevitable. His new wife was young and naturally had wanted her own family.

In the first few months, she knew how hurt the children had been, in particular her daughter. Fortunately she had gone off to study, and that changed her life pattern, but she and her brother had learned to cope with life differently, each in their own way. She had often thought that their son hoped that things would improve and that she and her husband may even get back together, but she had told him not to daydream and get on with life. How often had she thought the same thing, but she could not bring herself to talk about it, even with Mama. No, it was over, and she had to move on. Time had been a great healer, and she had done many of the trips she had promised herself, but always hoping that they may meet up one day and perhaps become friends again, at least for the children's sake. They had been married over twenty years, and she knew him well. *He will call*, she told herself, *just be patient. Dinner first, then who knows, there may even be time for dessert!*

He called her late the following morning. She answered immediately, wondering if it was he.

"Hello there," he said. "How is madame this morning?"

"Just fine," she laughed, "and how about yourself? Oh and by the way, congratulations on the baby girl."

"Thanks," he replied, preferring to add no further comment on the matter of his daughter. "I wondered if you would be free for dinner, perhaps tomorrow evening?"

"I think that will be possible," she answered, her heart beginning to pound.

"Anywhere special you would care to dine?"

"No, why don't you surprise me? You know that I always loved surprises."

If he had any doubt about her coming, these words proved otherwise.

"So, a surprise it will be," he laughed. "Why don't I pick you up around19.30?"

"I'll be ready," she told him.

"Until then, take care," he said, and then in a softer tone, he added, "I am looking forward to our dinner date."

"Are you?" she said. "Then I am glad." She did not dare add that she too was looking forward to their date. It worried her and, at the same time, excited her. So, better say nothing, she thought.

As she placed the phone down, her mind turned to what she was going to wear the following evening. It should be sexy and sophisticated, but not too daring. *I think that a trip into town might just be warranted for such an occasion,* she thought, smiling. *The dress has to be right!*

It was not long before she found the dress she was looking for: a pure silk wrapover in a deep blue shade, almost the colour of her eyes. The dress had a fairly deep cleavage, a style she wore well, and she did not think it would shock even him. After all, she liked it and that was what mattered. It had a skirt that swirled gently as she moved, and the length was just right for showing off her still trim legs. She bought a new pair of high heels, something she definitely did not need. *But to hell with it*, she thought, *I am having fun*. She indulged in a new bottle of perfume and some bright lipstick and made an appointment at the hairdresser's for the next day.

When she returned home, she took the dress out of the bag and saw that it was just perfect. *Let's see what he has to say about it*, she thought with a touch of nostalgia.

Her ex-husband had booked a table at one of the finest hotels, one she liked, and he knew that their restaurant was first class. He so needed the evening to go well, to be somehow special and he knew that a lot of this depended on him. He knew that she could be flirtatious, if she was in the right mood, but he knew her well and knew that she may also be on the defensive, something he wished to avoid. He had felt slightly guilty at telling his wife that he had another business dinner the following evening. Business associates had arrived unexpectedly in town, he had said, and he had to take them out. She nodded and had handed him his daughter for her kiss before going down for the night. She did not say a lot these days, he thought after she left the room to take the baby upstairs. She was rather quiet and withdrawn, but he had put this down to the fact that the baby took up great deal of her time.

Even he had been surprised at her rapid acceptance of his excuse, one he knew he could use anytime, but she had not seemed to care or ask if he wished that she join him. He wondered if she had heard any gossip from the chauffeur or the security guard; it hardly seemed likely, he thought, but then she saw the guard a great deal during the day and something may have come up in a conversation.

The next evening, he picked her up at around 19.30. He knew the area she now lived; his son had told him many things about their new home, and it was not long before he found himself parked outside. She was watching him from the upstairs landing, and he got out of the car and walked towards the gates of the house. She noticed that he was dressed up for the evening out, in a dark-coloured suit with a white shirt and blue tie. She was suddenly happy that she had bought a new dress for the dinner. He rang the bell and took a step back; she opened the door, and as he looked at her admiringly, he said, "Shall we go?"

"Just let me get my handbag," she replied quickly.

He noticed that she had not invited him in, and he did not wish to take the initiative of just walking into the hallway, assuming that he had every right to do so. He did, however, notice from what he could see that the hall was ultra modern, with the walls and doors painted in white and cream. The floors were oak, he thought, and a Persian carpet had been carelessly thrown over the shining wood which gleamed in the light.

"You have a lovely home," he told her politely.

"I like it, and it suits my needs and my present lifestyle," she replied. Sensing that perhaps she been a little too outspoken, she added, "I had to find somewhere that felt like home, but you know that don't you? Perhaps one day you can drive over and I will show you around." He said no more on the subject.

He opened the car door for her; she got in and they made their way into town. Neither said very much, both perhaps waiting for the other to lead into a particular subject, whilst both wishing to avoid particular subjects.

Upon arriving at the restaurant, he left his car to be parked, and they walked in together. To any onlooker, they looked the perfect couple, both handsome and expensively dressed.

They were shown to their table; the maitre d'hôtel had seen to it that they had a quiet corner table, something he had requested as being important. The table was laid with a white starched tablecloth and matching napkins. The crystal was clean cut and the cutlery polished to an amazing silver glow. The only decoration was a single rose in a white vase.

They sat down and were asked if they would care for an aperitif.

"A Kyr aux framboises, please," she said.

"And you, sir?"

"I shall have a glass of champagne," he answered.

If she was slightly taken aback at his request, she made no outward sign and instead gave him a warm smile.

"You know that you look lovely," he told her.

"Thank you," was all she said.

The maitre d'hôtel arrived with their drinks, before anything else could be said. They raised their glasses and looked at each other, neither speaking, just reading into each other's eyes. She wondered just how much he had changed, but at the same time, how far he was prepared to go. She looked up from her glass, thinking that he had spoken to her whilst she had been lost in her own thoughts. "Sorry, did you say something?" she asked, widening her eyes.

Her eyes never failed to touch him. He, who had seen many pretty eyes, could never seem to find a pair to match hers. As she looked right at him, he felt as though he were drowning in their intensity and depth. He knew then that he wanted her back; the warmth of the room made him feel almost claustrophobic. It could be the champagne, although he knew that was not the cause of how he was feeling at this exact moment.

"Have you chosen yet?" she asked.

"I am going to have smoked salmon with avocado, and then why don't we share the dorade baked in sea salt? You always liked that."

"Good idea, let's order."

He chose bisque de homard for a starter, and after the meal was ordered, the sommelier arrived with the wine list.

"How about continuing with champagne?" he asked.

"Fine, and perhaps a bottle of still water."

The matter of the menu being settled, he took her hand in his. She neither flinched nor withdrew, but he sensed that she was not totally at ease. He felt a little clumsy and laughed at his lack of seduction power, at least where his exwife was concerned. How many men had held her hand over these past few years? How many lovers had she taken? The idea did not appeal to him; he found it rather disquieting.

She sat watching his face and knew more or less what was going through his mind. He was thinking about her, but exactly what, she had no idea.

She asked him about the baby, thinking this may be a secure enough ground to start with.

"Oh, she is just fine, getting bigger every day, but then they do that, don't they?"

"Who does she look like?" she asked softly.

"Perhaps more like me, at least the upper part of the face, but she does have her mother's mouth."

He knew that she was trying to keep the conversation light and could not blame her. Did he really think that he could just walk back into her life again and that all would be forgiven and forgotten? Their starters arrived, and they both said, "Bon appétit," simultaneously.

At that moment, the chill around that corner table left, and soon they were chatting like old friends, friends who had not seen each other for a long time and who had plenty of catching up to do. They spoke about their pride in their children, especially their son, who was doing so well at university. "Looks as though he is turning into a real Brit," he said with laughter. "By the way, he is coming round to see the new baby soon; he wants to see who she looks like."

"Who does she look like?" she asked him gently.

"Oh, I think she has a fair bit of both of us, but the hair is certainly mine. She is going to be dark like our daughter and, I hope, just as pretty," he added, smiling

Their daughter took up quite a bit of their conversation too. She was presently taking some time away from college, working on a project, and appeared to be putting mind and soul into this task.

"She has matured a great deal, you know," she told him. "A good thing perhaps, it was maybe time she learned that life is not always a bed of roses."

"You have always been a little too hard on her, but then, she did need some handling," he admitted.

They continued talking throughout dinner, until she announced that she was popping out to the powder room. While she was away, he took out his mobile and phoned home. He told his wife that the business dinner was going well and that they still had a few topics to discuss over dessert. Then he would be making his way home.

"Don't wait up for me," he told her.

When his exwife reappeared, she told him she thought it was getting rather late and that maybe he ought to be thinking about returning home to his family.

He looked at his watch; she was right, the evening was now drawing to a close, and it was time to drive her home. He called for the bill and they left the restaurant, stopping only to collect her coat. The car was brought round, and he wondered, as he opened the door for her, if he would be invited in. She too was thinking of the best manner in which to end such a lovely evening. She knew it would be unwise of her to invite him for a nightcap, as she feared that the situation could quickly get out of hand, and she did not wish to move too quickly. She was not yet ready to make that final move but if this evening's signals were correct, the feeling was reciprocated. But it was way too soon to think of romance again. She thought that if they let the barriers down now, only hurt and disappointment would be awaiting both of them, but certainly her.

While driving her home, he too was thinking along the same lines. Perhaps she was prepared to forgive him a little, but she was not yet ripe to explore a new adventure with him. He had to be careful and take this second chance, if that what it was, step by step. They finally reached their destination, and before letting her out of the car, he leaned over and gave her a peck on the cheek.

"Thanks for a wonderful evening," she said. "I shall be going off next week for a couple of short trips, but why do we not keep in touch?"

Smiling affectionately at her, he said that he would ring her in a couple of week's time. This would give them both some time to think things over, something they both needed.

Arriving home, he parked the car in the garage and made his way into the silent house. He quietly went upstairs, changed, and washed before making his way to the baby's room. She was sound asleep and did not move as he kissed her lightly on her forehead.

In the bedroom, his wife too appeared to be sleeping as he slipped in beside her. She was lying on her side, and he listened to her steady breathing in the silence of the night. He was glad that she was asleep, thus avoiding any questions relating to his evening.

She was, in fact, not asleep. She had heard him come in and had thought it better to feign sleep. As he approached the bed, she thought that she could perceive the faintest tinge of perfume.

A tear silently rolled down her cheek; she prayed that sleep would come soon. He lay still, picturing that smile, the softness of her lip, a mouth just waiting to be kissed.

He lay dreaming and for a moment imagined that she was there standing at the foot of his bed. He looked again; she was there but just out of his reach. He knew that it was wishful thinking and that the light reflecting from outside in the garden was playing tricks with his mind.

He soon fell asleep and, for the first time in many years, did not take the time to pray.

THE SON'S STORY

He had been living in the university campus in the UK for almost two years now.

He had applied to study at this particular university and had been overjoyed when the acceptance letter dropped through the mailbox early one morning.

The year leading up to his final exams at school had not been an easy one. Sometimes he had only been happy when playing football or engrossed in his history books. The sport relieved him of a great deal of anger and stress, much of which had come from his parents' separation and divorce.

Life had changed considerably after the divorce. He knew that it had been a bitter one but was unaware of all the details; the only thing he was sure of was that it had been very hard on his mother. He had chosen to go and live with her. Together, they had found a new house, a little farther away from the city, but still only a twenty-minute train ride to school. He could not have envisioned living in their "old" home with his father and new wife. No, that had never been a question, and his father had accepted his choice without any remark.

He did not hate his father, unlike his sister, who had made her feelings more than clear. She was away studying, making a new life for herself. He often wondered if she ever chose to remember who paid for her expensive college, her apartment, not to mention her credit card bills each month. She should be a little more understanding and forgiving he often thought, but then she had always been spoiled. The fact that their father had remarried someone only a few years older than his sister had enraged her. He thought sometimes it could have been more jealousy than hatred. She could be very selfish and attention seeking at times, and although their mother had never taken her tantrums, he knew that his father had always given in to her every whim.

Life with Mum in their new abode was not hard. She gave him plenty of freedom, but he liked to think that he was there for her, sheltering her from all the hurt and disappointment, not to mention the gossip he had heard around town concerning his parents' split. It was she who had encouraged him to post his application to study away from home. She had told him that when he was accepted, as she was sure he would be, she was planning on taking a long break, well overdue.

"Just think," she had told him, "I am free to do exactly as I please now. Don't you start worrying about me; things are going to be just fine."

He had, in the end, believed her. She was strong, and he loved her so. He had been told often at school that his mother was a "wow mum," and he had come to realize that. He was very proud of her and remembered the pair of them celebrating with champagne the day he had received his entrance results.

Regarding his father, they had reached an agreement whereby he would visit him every two weeks, going to the house after school and staying for dinner. To begin with, he had argued about these visits, telling his mother that he did not feel comfortable about going.

"I feel as though I am one person too many at the table," he had told her after one of his visits.

"Nonsense," she had argued. "He is your father, after all, and you know he loves you very much."

He had continued, "But the house is not the same anymore."

"Well, it can't be," his mother answered. "We have a new home here, and shortly you will be heading off to start your studying, so for the time being, the visits continue."

He knew then that she had won and decided not to raise the subject again. Two months later, it was time to pack his case and head off to start his studies and a fresh beginning. He had gone to say good-bye to his father and his wife (or "the other woman," as his sister liked to call her).

"She's a witch," she had told him on the phone more than once, "and don't ever forget that," adding the last phrase as if to emphasise once more her contempt of her father's new marriage.

In a strange way, his sister's image of his father's new wife was not exactly accurate; she was nothing like the person she tried to portray. He found the young woman rather lost and lonely and obviously unaccustomed to having servants around her; this he had noticed very quickly. She became almost like a shadow in the background when he visited, and he often wondered where his father had met this girl. He had never dared to ask and had never been told.

One thing he gave her credit for was the fact that she had never attempted to become friends with him. She treated him with a certain reserve, without trying to put forth a hand of friendship. He liked this; he would not have known how to react if she had done otherwise. She was always polite and never forgot to ask him how his studies were going or if he had won a certain football game. He was old enough to realise that his father was in love with her and vice versa. He knew all about sexual attraction and thought that at least they were both happy with one another.

Around eight months into their marriage, she had taken to wearing a headscarf over her dark blonde hair.

He had wondered why. Surely his father had not requested her to do this. He knew that she had converted to Islam prior to the wedding, more than likely to please his father. He was aware that his mother had never converted and neither he nor his sister had ever attended the mosque. He thought of his sister's long, dark, glossy hair and her abundant collection of miniskirts and dresses; no, it could not be his father's wish for her to dress in this manner. She also chose to wear rather plain clothes, which made her look much older than her years; it was as though she did everything possible to look plain and dowdy, the exact opposite to his mother and sister. He and his father had never spoken of religion, although he knew that he neither drank alcohol nor smoked and would not permit any alcohol in the house. At meal times it had always been water or fruit juice on the table. The fact that his mother now loved champagne made him wonder if his father had forbidden her to drink alcohol. Now that she was free, she gladly drank a glass of wine with friends and was always happy to open the champagne bottle when there was something special to celebrate.

When Grandma had come to stay with them shortly after they moved into the house, they had opened quite a number of bottles, and he had been allowed to join in the fun; perhaps it had been the bubbles which had made the party seem fun, as the atmosphere then had been anything but joyful.

He continued his packing and his mind flashed back, this time to the wedding.

There had been few guests present; he had gone, not out of choice but more out of duty. His sister had refused to attend, and he felt he owed this one favour to his father. Of course there had been his paternal grandparents, his father's three brothers and their wives, and his aunt. There had been also a business associate who attended along with his new wife. Nobody had been there from the bride's side, something he found rather strange.

The wedding ceremony had been short and fairly simple. His father had worn a long white cotton robe, and his bride wore a long mauve dress. She had bracelets on both her wrists, and her ankles were also adorned with jewels. She wore long dangling earrings, and on her head she wore a purple transparent veil with pearl beads on the top, most likely to keep the veil in place, or so he thought. He remembered his mother and sister asking him how she had been dressed for the ceremony. This was all he could tell them, being neither fashion conscious nor particularly interested in the subject.

His father had presented his bride with a large diamond ring and had told his son during the reception that this wedding was "a weaving together of two souls and two destinies."

Suddenly he was brought back to reality, hearing his roommate shouting from down the corridor to him to hurry up, as dinner was now ready and that pizzas do not wait for anyone!

He was suddenly hungry and happy, he thought, making his way down to his friend's room.

He had just been chosen to play for the university football team; the trainer had told him that morning that he would be playing a midfield position. This was partly due to his medium height, and also the trainer had praised him, saying that he was pretty gifted with his passing. He had added that his free kicks and penalties were carried out with precision and that he liked the accuracy of his shots. These facts put together were now giving him the chance to play for his university colours. This pleased him as much as the knowledge that he had also passed his recent exams with flying colours.

The past term, he had concentrated on studying Benjamin Disraeli (1804-1881). He had learned that although born into a Jewish family, he had been baptised into the Church of England at the age of thirteen. This intrigued and fascinated him. He had never much thought about religion, other than knowing his father was a Muslim. He wondered if he should attend the Islamic meetings he knew were held in the university; many of the established Muslim students went to them. He however had never gone to any of these meetings, preferring to stay more neutral with the other students and not being pointed out as a "foreigner" or a "religious fanatic." He knew that he was certainly not the latter and took Islam as just another way of life, but if he were made to choose, would he follow in his father's steps or find the courage to search for another religion, one that he alone had chosen?

Disraeli had certainly taken this step, and he had also taken time as a young student to travel Europe and then on to the East. In 1827, he had written *Vivien Grey*, and although not his most famous book, it was followed by the far more well-known *Sybil* and *The Two Great Nations*.

Finally, Disraeli had entered Parliament in 1837. His maiden speech was not a great success, but he took no offence, stating simply, "The time will come when you will hear me." He was sure he would have liked this man; his integrity, ambition, and will to succeed had made him a truly great statesman. History had shown that he had made the second reform act in 1867, giving all householders in the boroughs the right to vote. Also, the act allowed all lodgers paying £10 and men paying £12 rent the right to vote for the first time. Lord Derby had called it "a leap in the dark." How wonderful, he thought, to have the ability to change men's lives by standing up for their rights and, more importantly, having the courage to do just that. It was down to a question of beliefs; how many questions came down to this basic fact? The various laws and reforms that had been passed had changed the face of Britain.

His next essay was to be based on another great British politician, the great liberal statesman Gladstone. From what he had already researched, this looked to be another powerful and interesting period in British history. He already knew that Gladstone's famous quote had been "My mission is to pacify Ireland," not a simple task, even today, he thought to himself. He looked forward to digging deeper into this prime minister's era and was certain that he was going to enjoy writing another essay which would stand him in good stead for next year. He had passed with good marks on Disraeli and hoped to be able to do the same on his next history exam.

British politics interested him. Their democratic system was one of the finest in the world and an example to many other countries; perhaps this is why he had wished to come and study here. *Maybe I could stand for Parliament one day,* he thought, laughing as he wondered what his father would think of such an idea.

His father had asked him on several occasions if he knew what he wished to do after he obtained his degree. He had no answer to that question, at least for the time being. He knew that his father would have liked him to study law, something worthwhile and appropriate. To his father, history pertained to the past; the subject was old news. He did not find this at all and loved his courses. *Law*, he thought, *is not a subject for me.*

Life had been pretty good over the past year. He had also managed to get to several motorbike rallies; his father had given him a Ducati for his eighteenth birthday, something he was very proud of.

After he finished dinner, he resumed his packing; he thought of seeing his mother again tomorrow and all the things they would have to say to one another. He was catching an early afternoon flight, and she had said she would be at the airport to collect him. He had also promised to pass by his father's home and see the baby daughter. He had bought her a little teddy; *not very original*, he thought, *but maybe this is the one thing she doesn't possess as yet!*

He thought again of his mother and knew that they would no doubt sit up half the night chatting, and she would be happy to hear all his good news. He also hoped to catch up with the young girl living a few doors further down the road. She was studying philosophy, and they had spoken several times together over coffee. She had introduced him to Nietzsche: his sad ending in an asylum in Switzerland, and his sister's struggle to have his works published after his death. She had told him in her last letter that she was now studying Sartre, a modern French philosopher; she enjoyed reading about his theories very much. However, philosophy was not the main reason he loved seeing her, and he hoped she knew that. After all, there was more to life than studying.

THE RECONCILIATION

She saw him in the arrival lounge as he came out of Customs. She thought how well he looked and was glad that he had finally settled down over the past year. She loved her son dearly and was looking forward to having him home for a week.

She waved to him, and he came running towards her; they hugged each other before making their way to the airport underground car park.

"So what's new, Mum?" he asked. "Anything exciting I should know about?"

"I'm just fine," she answered, "and by the way, congratulations yet again on your excellent examination results."

"Thanks Mum; now tell me, are we going straight home or do you want to stay in town for dinner?"

"We are going home, I have prepared your favourite pasta dish, and there is salad for starters."

"It's really great being back again; you know that I don't get fed like that at university."

His mother laughed before replying, "Well, just don't think that you are about to get spoiled every night."

They arrived at the house, and he took his rucksack out of the boot after his mother put the car away in the garage.

Once they were both inside, and after several moments, she asked him casually, "Have you spoken to your father recently?" As she asked this, she took a bottle of Chablis from the fridge.

"Yep," he said, "and he sounded pretty pleased with my results too; also, I have been chosen to play for the university football team, which I think will make him happy too.

"I got the little one a teddy; what do you think about that?"

His mother just laughed and said she was sure that the gift would be much appreciated.

"Now let's talk about you," she said, "and catch up with what you have been doing. I am very proud that you have made the football team. I can imagine that your father will also be very pleased. So let's have a toast to your success." As she said this, she poured out some wine for each of them.

Later he went up to his room and unpacked; he shouted down that he going for a shower before supper.

"Fine," she said, "I'll prepare the table; take your time."

As she began setting the table, she wondered how she was going to approach the subject of their reconciliation. He did not know as yet that she had been seeing his father again, or that she had asked him over the following evening for a meal. She was not certain that he could have coped with all this on his first evening home, but she planned to break the news later on over dinner.

She hoped that her son would be pleased, but then she could not be sure. She had said nothing to her daughter, who was always plaguing her with questions about new boyfriends and asking if she was seeing anyone special. *A little more time is needed when dealing with her*, she thought; she and her father were now on speaking terms and saw one another now and again, but she did not wish to giver either of her children false hopes. She herself had no idea which path she was treading, but she hoped that her son's reaction would be favourable.

He suddenly appeared from upstairs, wearing his jeans and a clean shirt.

"I'm starving," he said, "how about you?"

"Me too," she replied, smiling. "Let's sit down and start."

"How's Grandma?"

"Doing really well and naturally looking forward to your visit this summer."

She thought that she would take the opportunity now.

"I've invited someone round for dinner tomorrow evening; do you think that you will be here?"

"Great," he said. "Sure, I can be here. Anyone I know?"

"It is actually," she said quietly. "It's your father."

She watched his face and saw disbelief followed by joy.

"Dad's coming round here? What's going on, Mum?"

She smiled and told him very casually that they had met by chance on her flight back from seeing Grandma.

"He just happened to be one of the passengers sitting near me."

"And?" he asked her.

"Well, nothing really, we got on fine; perhaps things were a little strained to begin with, but they've improved in the past few weeks. I thought it would be nice if he came round tomorrow evening while you are here."

"That's great, but what about his wife and the new baby?"

"Let's not jump the gun," she told him. "We have only had dinner a couple of times, and for your information, he has never been in this house."

"Mum, are you still in love with him?" he asked.

"I don't know, son," was all she could say.

He looked at her and knew that she was still in love with his father. He only hoped that she was not going to be hurt again; tomorrow evening would give him a chance to see his parents together, and perhaps only then would he understand what was going on.

"What about Sis? Does she know anything about this?"

"No, I do not think it very wise; after all, there is nothing to tell her."

"Fine, my lips are sealed," he replied. "Now let's finish the salad so we can start on your pasta, it smells good, if that is what I smell coming from the kitchen."

As his mother left the table to see to see how things were progressing, he sat back in his chair, a glass of red wine in hand, and wondered if his father was thinking of leaving his wife to return home with Mum. Her comment had come as quite a surprise to him, and he knew that she had tried to keep the news casual, probably for his sake, but was there going to be another divorce, and what about the baby? He wondered if his mother had similar thoughts.

She appeared from the kitchen with a piping hot bowl of carbonara pasta.

"Let's eat while it is still hot," she said.

He poured her a glass of Chianti and refilled his own glass.

"To tomorrow evening then," he said.

His mother looked at him while she drank her wine slowly; savouring the taste as she quietly repeated his words, "Yes, to tomorrow evening."

They finished their meal with idle chit-chat, after which he retired for the evening.

His father arrived the next evening at around seven o'clock. He watched as his father parked the car and made his way up to the front door. He noticed that he was casually dressed in a pair of black jeans with a blue-and-white checked shirt. He also noticed that he was carrying a small bouquet of pale pink roses, his mother's favourite. He opened the door, not giving his father time to ring. They put their arms around each other, and the son said, "Nice to see you again, Dad. How are things?"

There was no awkwardness, something which relieved him; he had been a little apprehensive about how his son would react to this visit.

The lady of the house appeared from the kitchen; she was also wearing a pair of jeans, a large white shirt open at the neck, and a pair of beige loafers. He thought how young she looked and also sensed that she appeared very happy at this family reunion. She thanked him for the flowers, turning back into the kitchen to put them in water and shouting to both of them to take a seat in the lounge.

As he entered the room, he thought how well she had decorated the place. There was a large marble fireplace on the centre wall with two beige sofas facing it. In the centre of the room was an ultra modern glass coffee table scattered, but with care, with a selection of fashion magazines and weekly periodicals. His eyes then took in the adjoining dining room; it, too, was of modern design. A large glass table sat in the centre of the room, and on the side wall was a white console with a vase of colourful flowers and several silver photo frames. The white walls were adorned with contemporary paintings, giving the room an instant vibrant flash of colour. He suddenly felt at home and liked the warm feeling the rooms gave him.

He turned from his thoughts as his son spoke.

"So Dad, this is quite a surprise, and it looks as though you like the place."

"I do, very much, and to answer your question, your mother's invitation this evening came as rather a surprise to me also. I was delighted with your results this term; you have certainly done well," his father told him.

They chatted on, quite at ease, discussing motorbikes, his good news about having been chosen for the football team, his sister; in fact, everything but the main topic.

"When you two have finished talking, how about opening the wine?" she called out from the kitchen.

"Shall we go and give her a hand?" his father asked.

"Why don't you go?" the son suggested. "Mum will be happy to have someone else rather than me around in the kitchen."

He walked into a gleaming kitchen designed entirely in black and white granite. The tiles on the walls were black, as was the free range cooker. The cupboards were white and the work surrounding entirely made in slabs of black granite, making it all look rather chic but friendly.

"I see that you have become quite domesticated," he told her almost lovingly.

"Let's say, I had no choice," she answered him, turning around from the oven. He wanted to put his arms around her and never let go but said nothing, preferring to pick up the tray lying on the kitchen table and carry it through to the lounge.

She arrived with the champagne, and they lifted their glasses.

"I think that this evening deserves a toast," the son told them both. "Just a pity that Sis is not here and the family would be complete."

They lifted their glasses and drank. She put on some music, a little light piano bar style which rather suited the event (if "event" was the correct word). Everything seemed to be going well so far, and she only hoped that it would continue that way for the rest of the evening.

She had come to realise over the couple of evenings they had spent in each other's company that she was happier than she had felt in a long time, and she knew that he felt the same. Neither of them had made any move to take their rekindled relationship any further than that of deep friendship, each being too frightened of rejection. That was one of the reasons she had never invited him into the house when he drove her home after dinner. She was aware of her feelings and knew that she could be so easily tempted back into having an affair, but she had preferred to take things slowly, thus giving him time also to understand his own feelings. There would be no hesitation, no pressure, no holding them back once they made a move to jump the last hurdle; the thought scared her.

Around nine o'clock, the son announced that he was popping out for a while; in actual fact, he was planning a visit to the young girl down the road. He was looking forward to seeing her again, and when he had phoned her earlier that afternoon, they had decided to meet up at her house for an ice cream. Knowing that his father was coming round, he also wanted to make an exit after an appropriate time, to give his parents a chance to be on their own, something he was sure they both wanted but obviously would never have suggested.

"See you later," he told them as he put on his jacket. "I guess that you will still be here when I get back, Dad?" he called out from the hall.

"I think I may well be," his father answered. "Depends of course on what time you plan to return," he added jokingly.

"Have fun," his mother shouted as she heard him open the front door.

As he walked down the street, he wondered if this could possibly be a new beginning for his parents.

They had certainly seemed at ease in each other's company, and he was glad that he had left when he had. *Who knows?* he thought quietly to himself. *I guess only time will tell what they are going to do.* They were like young teenagers, neither wishing to make the first move. Finally he kissed her and she responded quickly. They both knew that now was the right moment.

She lay on her bed with only a peach-coloured silk gown over her body. He kissed her gently, delighting in the smell of her fragrance. He hesitantly kissed her breasts while smoothly sliding down the satin straps of her gown. Then he kissed her stomach and waited. She arched her back, and as the gown slid off her body, he gently slid in between her legs. She laughed with joy as he seductively began making love to her, very gently at first, perhaps still afraid that she would pull away at the last moment. Tonight there would be no depth to the pleasure he wished to give her, tonight there would be no limits, the barriers were now down, and she was his again. Tonight was theirs for the taking.

THE BETRAYAL

She would have been unable to tell anyone the day she had started hating him.

She had guessed for several months now that he was seeing someone else, of that she was sure. She had tried to put it to the back of her mind, telling herself that she was wrong, that it was all in her imagination, but the seed of doubt grew within her until it flowered into certainty.

She began to understand how his first wife must have felt. Up until now she had never given the matter much thought, but now she knew only too well how hurt she must have been; now she was experiencing the same feeling. The clock had turned fully, and it was now her turn to experience the feeling of total loss and despair.

His rejection of her was like a river never ending, a tidal wave engulfing her soul. In other words, it was something she was powerless to control or to stop.

The deep love she had always had for him began to ebb, slowly but surely, although it took several months for her to die internally.

She, who had done everything to win his love, to keep his love, now knew that she had lost it. She, who had taken him away from his family, knew that she was paying the highest price, his betrayal.

He had told her the previous week that he wanted to sit down and talk; she wondered if he had guessed that she knew he was seeing another woman, but she could not have anticipated what he was about to tell her that evening. A girlfriend was what he was going to tell her, but she waited until he began to speak. The words she was hearing almost suffocated her: he was returning back to his first wife, he was leaving her and the baby. His words were brutal, and he had done nothing to take the cutting edge off the bitter words.

This had been the hardest part, hearing that he was leaving her to return home, that he should never have married her and now wanted a divorce. The blow could not have been harder if he had slapped her. She thought her brain was about to burst as the thumping within it seemed to intensify with each word he spoke. She could feel her heart sinking, like a stone thrown down an endless pit;, she now knew that there would be no assistance back to daylight.

He had moved out that same evening, and in a way she was glad. She could not have borne seeing him on a daily basis. He called regularly to see how the baby was doing, and his son had popped around to see them. She did not know exactly what he knew about the situation and did not ask him. He had stayed for a coffee, like he had done several times over the past few months, and as always he enjoyed playing with his half sister. She had even received a card from his elder daughter, congratulating them on the birth of the little one, and she had even sent her a picture of the baby. How could she have ever thought such a thing would happen?

She had been so sure of his love and had even thought that with his two elder children they could start becoming a family; she had no hope that they would accept her into their hearts, but she had thought that they might just accept her as their father's new wife. They both seemed to like the baby, and she had hoped in time that they might even grow to love her. How could she ever have been so stupid and so naive? The future had begun to look brighter, and she had so hoped that he would love her again like he had in the past. But that was not to be. These had all been fantasies in her dream, while all this time, he had been planning to leave her and the baby.

And so she began to hate him; it commenced with a span of darkness which spread through her system like a sickly poison. No pain, only darkness; no glimmer of hope that he may change his mind. She knew him too well. There could be no hope, therefore, that the poison could eventually be extracted from her body like the venom of a snake. No, she hated him with a hatred she did not know anyone could possess.

It was then that the idea came to her. To begin with it, seemed impossible, but as each week passed and her hatred grew, she finally understood what she had to do. She could not and would not hesitate in carrying her plan out, and the baby had to go with her. This was one of the most important parts of her plan. She knew from her classes on Islam that to sacrifice one's life for a good reason ensured the right to sit at Allah's side.

She had to act quickly. He had left the house nearly three months ago. Where he was lodging, she had no idea and had not plucked up the courage to ask him. She knew deep down that she was too afraid to learn that he had returned to his first wife. All important matters relating to their daughter were arranged through his lawyers. It had been set up that he would have the baby every weekend, collecting her on Saturday mornings and returning at around six o'clock Sunday evenings, and that she would have her throughout the entire week.

She had agreed to this arrangement, in the interim, knowing that his lawyers would contradict her if she ever attempted to deny him his parental right. It was his daughter also, the lawyers had told her, while, as if to pacify her, implying that after the divorce, she would be extremely well looked after financially. In other words, she could start a new life for herself with a substantial settlement in the bank. How little they knew of her or her life, treating her as if she were someone who could be paid off, rather like a bad debt.

They had also told her that the current arrangements regarding the baby's custody would most likely remain in place for several months until divorce proceedings were held. At that time, other plans would be drawn up. She knew instantly what that meant. He would get full custody. No, she did not see her future like this at all; in fact, she had other ideas, but those she kept to herself.

While working out her own plan, she sometimes wondered what his reaction would be when they broke the news to him. Would it be one of amazement or one of grief? Perhaps even both. There would naturally be horror, due to the fact that she had taken the baby with her on her last and final flight.

As if to justify her idea, she told herself that he had asked for all of this and deserved what she was scheming. She had to make him suffer and knew that he would, if she could only go through with it.

Somehow in all this distress, she told herself that he had loved her, once. She had been there for him when he had needed someone. Had he not left his family for her? So why now had he decided to change everything and turn his back on her? Had he not been proud of her when she had converted to Islam, when she had participated in the period of Ramadan with him and the joy of having the baby? She knew that he had not really wanted to start a new family but was certain that he loved his daughter.

She was on very unsure ground and had no artillery to fire in this war; she had lost before the battle had even begun. She let a tear drop down from her eye to her mouth. She felt the salt in her mouth, and the taste made her cry a little more. She felt no guilt at what she was about to do; he would be left with the guilt, and her sins would be absolved. That would be her justice and his life sentence.

She had three more weeks to finalize her plans. He was going away next month on a business trip, and it would be the perfect timing for her and the baby to also go on a trip, a long and peaceful journey that would take them to a better place. Where they were going, there would be only joy and happiness. She knew for certain that her sorrow and grief would be left here on earth.

Part III

"Children begin by loving their parents, after a time they judge them; rarely, if ever, do they forgive them."

Oscar Wilde, 1854-1900

THE NEWS FALLS

The police now had a difficult task; the main priority was to find out the identity of the young lady who had died so horrifically in the fire with her baby. They had gone back into the restrooms and found a handbag, possibly belonging to the young woman, who had been taken away a few moments ago in the ambulance.

They searched through it and came across a passport. From the passport, they found her name and address; they also found a telephone number which could be possibly that of her husband, to contact in case of emergency.

They decided to call the telephone number. A young lady answered the phone, and they asked to speak to the person whose name they had in front of them. A few seconds later, another female voice came on the phone; it was the chairman's PA. The policeman leading the inquiry once more asked to speak to the name he had in front of him.

"May I ask who is calling?" the PA asked, and the policeman identified himself without explaining what had happened.

The PA wondered why the police would be asking for the chairman; it seemed to her rather unusual, not to say strange.

"I am sorry," she replied, "but he is away on business at the moment. Perhaps I can assist or take a message for him?"

"I am afraid not," the policeman replied. "It is very important that we speak to the gentleman himself; can you provide us with a contact number where we may reach him?"

She hesitated, knowing that the chairman did not like anyone giving out his private mobile phone number, but as this appeared to be an emergency, she thought she had better do as requested and proceeded to give the officer his number. He thanked her and said nothing further. Putting down the phone, she wondered what could be important enough for the police to call the office. She hoped that there had not been an accident and wondered if a member of his family had come to harm. She called down to the receptionist who had passed her the call and asked her who the police had requested to speak to.

"Was it the chairman?" she asked.

"It was, that is why I passed the call up to you," the young girl replied. "Was that okay?"

"Of course," the PA answered.

She once again put down the phone down, this time with more uneasiness. Something was wrong, and she did not really know what to do. She made herself a coffee and decided to call the PR. He would surely know what all this was about. She knew that he had accompanied the chairman yesterday afternoon to visit an air show for a couple of days. She dialled his mobile, and he answered the phone immediately.

"Hi," she said. "How are things?"

"Fine," he told her. "You sound worried, what's up?"

She told him about the call and asked if he had seen the boss that morning.

"Yes, I have," he said, "we had breakfast together, and he is now up in his room preparing some papers before we leave for the show. The driver should be here soon. Is there anything I can do?"

"I doubt it," she answered. "Perhaps I am just overreacting; however I do have an uneasy feeling that there is something not quite right.

They said good-bye, and the PR manager looked at his watch, thinking that the driver would be there at any moment. He found the call to the office from the police rather disturbing and understood the PA being a little anxious. There must be something wrong, he thought. He saw the chairman come out of the lift, and his first thought was, *Oh my God*. His boss's face was ashen and devastated with grief, almost horror.

He walked across to him and asked if he was feeling all right.

"I was just speaking with the police," he told him.

He knew then that only bad news was about to follow. In fact, it suddenly dawned on him that he was about to hear some awful news and he was filled with dread.

"It appears that my wife may have committed suicide," he continued. "Can you please call the house guard and pass him on to me?"

The PR manager quickly dialled the guard's mobile at the villa and passed him to the chairman.

"Did you see my wife this morning?" he heard him ask the security guard.

What the answer was, he did not know, but his boss collapsed into a nearby sofa in the reception. He called out for water and quietly took the phone away from him.

The guard was still on the line.

"What's going on?" he asked the guard. "Is there a problem?"

"I don't know," the guard answered. "The boss asked if I had seen his wife this morning, and I told him that she had left for the airport a couple of hours ago by taxi. I offered to drive her but she told me that she was planning to meet a friend. She had the baby with her, and I thought it strange that she did not want a lift, but she insisted on going by herself. Is something wrong?"

The PR did not know what to answer but told him not to worry, and that he would be in touch again later on in the morning.

He turned around to look at his boss again, and before he had time to say anything, the chairman reiterated, "I think perhaps that my wife is dead and the baby too."

The PR maanger could not believe what he was hearing and would have asked him to repeat what he had just said, except he could see the desperate look in the chairman's eyes; he could tell he had just been given devastating news. Only terrible news could give anyone such a haunted look.

"Drink some more water" was all he could say, wondering what the hell he should do now. His boss was the priority, and in one way or another, it was imperative that he get him back home again, as quickly as possible. He called the pilot and asked to reschedule the trip; there had been a change in plan and the chairman had to return urgently. What would be the earliest take-off time? The captain said that he could be ready to take off in three hours. The PR confirmed that this would be fine and said that they would be leaving the hotel within the next hour.

He then turned his attention to the man sitting next to him, slumped in a chair.

"The plane will be ready for takeoff in three hours," he told him. "I have a few calls to make and then will meet you down here in the lobby. Is there anyone you wish me to phone or contact in the meantime?"

"No," his boss replied. "I shall go up to my room, make some calls myself, collect my bags, and meet you down here in, say, forty-five minutes."

"Fine," his PR manager replied. "Do you wish me to call the office?"

"No thanks, I shall do that in due time," the chairman replied. "I shall have to contact my PA, once I am certain of the facts, but this I have to do personally, you understand?"

"Of course I do, just let me know if I can be of any assistance, no matter what."

Leaving the lobby, the PR then went outside, where he lit a cigarette and thought over the past ten minutes. What he had heard seemed unbelievable, and yet, in some way, it was very possible. He knew that there had been some rumours recently within in the office that his boss had been seeing his exwife. He knew nothing of this and took it to be nothing more than gossip. He had thought at the time that it was most unlikely, especially after the hostile divorce, but could it be possible that the rumour had been true? He wondered. What else could have made her do such a thing? Had the police even been certain that it was her before phoning the office? Why had they had not visited in person if they were sure? All these facts raced through his mind, while at the same time trying to come to terms with what he had heard. Surely it must be a mistake. He could not envision the chairman's new wife even thinking of taking her own life, never mind that of the baby too. No, surely it had been a misunderstanding, and the police had gotten the identities mixed.

He strolled along the pavement for a while and refrained from calling the office. It was not his place, and he did not wish to alarm anyone of uncertain facts that even he was not sure of.

He walked back into the hotel and made some calls, cancelling a luncheon and a subsequent meeting. He gave no reasons, only stating that the chairman had to get back home urgently.

As promised, the chairman appeared at the given time. He still looked stunned, but the colour had now returned to his cheeks, he was glad to see. Their driver arrived and took them directly to the airport, where the Learjet was awaiting them. They climbed into the plane, only stopping to greet the pilot. Nothing more was said on the subject until the chairman switched on his i-Pad. There, in front of them both, was the breaking news of the day:

"Woman and baby die in suicide furnace"

The PR sat listening to the news; he wanted to switch the computer off, but he sat there quietly, as his boss listened intently to every word that was being pronounced by the broadcaster. He knew that he was powerless to help him in any way, and so left him to listen attentively.

It was not a long flight, and soon they were back. The chairman told him just as they were about to descend that the police would be waiting for them; they would be taken straight out of the airport into an awaiting van. He could only nod his head in agreement, words failing him.

The police were indeed waiting for them as they disembarked from the plane. They were both taken away, no Customs, no Immigration, straight to the hospital morgue.

"Have you any further news?" he heard the chairman ask a police officer when they reached the hospital.

"No sir," he replied. "We are still in the early stages of our investigation."

"But you do think that it is my wife and baby?" he asked.

"We do, sir, but need your formal identification before we go any further into this matter. Once you have formally identified the bodies as being your wife and baby daughter, we can get forensics working on the case."

"Can I see them straight away?" he asked.

"You most certainly can, sir, but I must warn you that they are both very badly burned, the baby in particular."

The PR manager watched as his boss put his head in his hands. He realised then that there was a strong possibility that the police knew that the bodies were those of the chairman's wife and baby. It was they who had died that morning, and he knew that his boss was thinking exactly the same thing.

The question was why? The PR wondered yet again what could have pushed this young woman to commit such a terrible act. Was it vengeance, he thought, but why? What was she trying to prove and to whom? *Too many questions*, he thought, *and no answers. We are not yet sure that it is she.*

They had stayed at the hospital for over an hour, an hour which to him had seemed as long as an entire day and night, until finally the chairman confirmed that it was indeed his family. It was his wife and baby who had died that morning. They had both died of severe third degree burns, caused by the furnace she had created; there had been no way that either of them could have survived such heat. The baby had not suffered; as for his wife, she probably had been conscious of the fact that she was dying, until her last breath. She had obviously planned her suicide well and had succeeded.

"I think we should get you home now," he told the chairman, "you badly need to rest."

He knew that the next few days would be unbearable for his boss and only wished that there was something he could do to help him. However, he knew within himself that there was nothing he could do to eradicate the pain and sorrow the man was now feeling.

The PR also knew that within the next few hours, the press would get hold of the story and would hound the office and the chairman to get a scoop. The television had already gotten the story, and soon the entire horrific event would be printed in all the papers.

He knew that his boss would be able to cope with all the pressure; he was a broken man now but had an inner strength unlike anyone the PR had ever known in his life. However, he was in deep shock right now, and so getting him home was a priority. He wondered about his other family; someone would have to announce this to his son and daughter before they heard it through the media.

As if reading his thoughts, the chairman looked at his PR and put his hands on his shoulders.

"Thank you for everything," he told him. "I could not have managed without you; now I need to make a call to my daughter and son. I have already called the office and spoken to my PA. She knows what to do, and I told her that I would be in at the office later on this afternoon."

"Do you think this is really wise?" he asked.

"Yes, it is, I must get some papers together, as I will be expected to make an announcement to the press later on this evening."

"Can I do this for you?" the PR asked gently.

"No, I have to do this on my own, as I have to tell my family personally. I do not wish them to get a shock upon reading the tabloids."

The PR remained silent, and together they walked towards the car that was awaiting them.

After giving the house address, the chairman spoke.

"I shall take a couple of hours rest and make a few phone calls. Meet me back here around five o'clock. Does that suit you?"

"Sure," the PR replied. "In the meantime, if you need anything, just give me a ring. I shall be at home for the rest of the afternoon also."

They were soon across the city, and it was not long before they arrived at the chairman's home.

How on earth is he going to manage? Should he be left on his own right now? Not an easy question to answer, but the PR knew that privacy was essential to this man now, and so they said their good-byes, arranging to meet later on in the afternoon.

MOTHER AND SON

In a strange way, both mother and son heard the news in the same manner.

The son had just finished his morning English literature class and was making his way up to his room. He decided to go to the canteen and grab a coffee and a sandwich; he had plenty of time between classes and thought he deserved the break. Things were going fine, and after returning from the break at his mother's, he had found to his surprise that he was actually glad about the turnaround in his parents' life. Where it would all end, he had no idea, but it appeared that they were continuing to see one another, and if his mother's voice on the phone was anything to go by, she was one happy lady.

The only worry he had, if you could call it a worry, was what his father would do with his new wife and baby. He knew that it would be pretty hard on his father to walk away from this new family, something he would certainly have to do if he planned to get back together with his mother. He doubted his mother would continue on in this relationship without some serious changes having to be made. He could not imagine her becoming the mistress; somehow, it did not ring true. Knowing her as he did, she would either take his father back for good or walk away from the situation.

Nobody was actually going to win, he thought to himself; someone had to be hurt, and he prayed that it would not be his mother yet again.

He understood why she had decided not to say anything to his sister; a wise choice, but he knew Sis well, and she would soon guess that something was up. She had already quizzed him on several occasions, asking if Mum had a new man in her life. He had said nothing but knew that it would not be too long until she caught on.

He was halfway through his sandwich in the canteen when he heard the news flash on the television:

"Young woman burns herself to death and takes baby girl with her in her flight."

Oh my God, he thought to himself, *who could do such a thing?* He continued eating, without paying too much attention to what was being read out on the news. As they continued showing flashes of the airport where it had all happened that morning, he looked up from his book and realised that it was the airport near his home. He suddenly stopped reading and listened more attentively to what was being said. It suddenly struck him that it could be someone the family knew, especially where the baby was concerned. At this moment, his mobile rang, and he took it out of his jacket pocket. He saw the number was his mother's. *She's up early this morning,* he thought to himself. *I wonder what she has to tell me; hope it's good news.*

He answered the phone straight away; before he could say anything, she asked, "Have you seen the news this morning?"

"I have just been watching it now," he told his mother. "Did you hear about the accident at the airport this morning? Can you imagine such a thing, Mum?"

"I can," she said. "This is the reason I am calling you. I just spoke to your father. It appears, though we are not certain, that it was your father's wife and baby that perished in the furnace this morning."

"Your father told me that he had been contacted by the police a short while ago. It appears that there was a bag left in the restrooms, and they found his business card within the contents. He called me to let me know and asked that I contact you as soon as possible. He is flying back this afternoon to identify the bodies; until then, we cannot be sure of anything."

"Why would she do such a thing?" he asked.

"I really don't know, son; let's wait and see what this afternoon brings."

"I shall get a flight home this afternoon," he said. "I want to be with you and Dad; I'll give you a call before taking off and let you know when I arrive. However, don't expect me until after six o'clock. What about Sis? Has someone called her?"

"Your sister is away for a long weekend and will not be back until tomorrow. However, let's wait until we have confirmation before calling her."

"Fine," he said. "And how about you Mum, are you okay?"

She did not reply, not knowing what to tell him. She too was shocked at the news and knew how hurt and devastated her exhusband had sounded on the phone. Had his new wife by any chance done this to punish him, to make him feel guilty about wanting to return to his first family? The idea did not bear thinking about, and she could not imagine for one moment that this could push someone over the brink, to commit such a horrific act. No, surely it had to be something else, but what? Now that she was gone and the baby too, would they ever know what had pushed her to take her own life and that of the baby? Perhaps she left a note in the house, she thought to herself; surely if it is her, she would leave an explanation as to why she had committed suicide. Normally people leave a note explaining their reasons for taking their own life; hopefully she had too.

On the other hand, it may not be her, she thought; there may be a simple reason for her bag being in the toilets. Perhaps she had forgotten it and had gone away; yes, that was right, it might not be her. The police had made an error and had called her ex, hoping for an explanation There surely had been one, but they would all have to wait until he arrived back later on today and had the terrible ordeal of identifying the bodies. She had wanted to go and meet him at the airport, to be with him in this terrible turmoil, but had thought it wiser not to go. This was something he had to do alone; she knew he was travelling with his PR and that he would take care of him ensuring that all the logistics were taken care of. The police would do the rest.

She put the phone down and sat with her head in her hands. She started to weep, gently at first, and then found herself sobbing. She did not know if she was crying for herself or for her exhusband; all she knew was that she was hurting badly. Things had been going so smoothly for all of them; perhaps they had not given enough thought to her and the baby. They had, if the truth be known, expected the new wife to react as she herself had done a few years ago, with sadness and dignity. Nothing could have prepared either of them for this sort of revenge, and revenge she felt it was. *However, let's wait and see*, she thought to herself. *Time will tell.* She dried her tears as she lifted the phone.

THE PERSONAL ASSISTANT, PART 2

It was a fairly warm day for the month of April as the PA made her way across the bridge to the office. There was still a slight breeze in the air, and she glad that she had decided, albeit at the last moment, to put on an overcoat.

The chairman was away on a business trip, and the office was pretty quiet, hence taking an extra half hour for lunch, as she planned to do that day, would not be a problem, she had thought.

She no longer saw her boss's exwife. She knew that the divorce had been a difficult one and that his wife had been pretty upset about the entire incident. She herself had not believed the news that he was having an affair with someone twenty younger than himself; what had possessed him to do such a thing, she had never worked out. She still missed her weekly luncheons with his first wife. They had become friends, and she would have liked to continue seeing her. They had seen one another after the divorce, but things had not been the same. She did not somehow feel at ease anymore and felt that this was reciprocated. They had less to say to one another, and although her boss had never actually come out and said anything, she got the message that he preferred that she left the past behind. He was too much of a gentleman to say anything, but she had understood, and so time went by and eventually they had ceased to meet up. She had gotten into her head the fact that she was not to be trusted anymore, and as their conversations became rather one sided, they had parted, promising to call one another but knowing perfectly well that this would not happen.

She had seen the new wife on several occasions when she had passed by at the end of the day to meet her husband. They had said very little to one another, neither knowing what to say. She had not really liked her, or rather had not taken to her, preferring to think that she was rather insipid and insignificant. She had even told her husband that she was like the second wife in *Rebecca*. Her husband had laughed at her imagination and told her not to be so silly. But that is what she thought, and nothing as yet had made her change her mind. However, she had to concede that she must have had a gleam in her eye or something to attract the chairman's attention and more so to make him fall in love with her and divorce his first wife. Still waters run deep, her husband had told her, and in this case she had to admit that he was correct.

She was not always up to date on all the office gossip, often hearing it several days later from the PR. However, she had learned that the majority of the staff at first found her to be rather pleasant and kind, but no more . . .

As she went up in the lift and headed for her office, she felt a slight shiver go through her. Being a little superstitious, she wondered what today was going to bring. Hopefully nothing, she told herself, laughing at her own stupidity. She made a tea and poured herself some juice before checking the mail and the answering machine for any important messages. She had bought the paper on the way to the office and thought that she might just glance through it before starting her day. When the chairman was away, it was her only chance to relax a little, and she did this in the mornings, preferring to come in a little later than usual and taking a break until around ten o'clock.

The morning passed fairly quickly, and it was nearly lunchtime when the phone rang. She knew immediately who was on the other end of the line and immediately asked him how he was and how the meetings were going. Previously, he had asked her if she could perhaps think about accompanying him on some of his more important meetings, to take notes and get to know some of his business colleagues. She had been more than happy with his suggestion and had told him that she would seriously think the matter over. The idea of travelling on one of these private jets actually quite excited her, plus she got on well with the PR and began to feel that she was making progress with this job. She had tried to carve out an interesting job for herself and this request had somehow flattered her and made her think that perhaps she was getting somewhere.

She was therefore rather taken aback when she heard his voice, a voice she knew only too well, speaking in an almost inaudible manner. She sensed that something was terribly wrong, as she thought she heard her boss say that there had been an accident.

"Sorry, did you mention an accident? What do you mean?" she asked, beginning to feel a little uneasy.

"I had a call from the police earlier this morning," he told her. "My wife committed suicide early this morning and took the baby with her."

Her mouth went dry, and she felt sick, although she had nothing in her stomach; the room seemed to turn in front of her as she lifted the juice to her mouth to wet her lips. She hoped that the wetness may assist in bringing some words to her parched throat; she felt her mind crossing in all directions but the one she wished to take.

Nothing came from her mouth as she attempted to speak.

"It will be on the news tonight," her boss continued in a whisper. "Are you all right?" he suddenly asked her gently.

"Yes," she managed to bring this single word out of her mouth.

"Why don't you sit down?" he said. "I shall continue."

She did just this, still shaking but ready to listen to whatever was about to be told to her.

"It will be on the news tonight," he repeated. "She blew herself up at the airport this morning and the baby too. Kindly assemble the staff and advise them that there has been a terrible accident. Please say nothing further. If you are contacted by the press or the television, please say nothing. I shall be flying back this afternoon and will take matters in hand."

"I am so sorry," she heard herself mumble.

"Thank you," he replied.

"I shall see you later on in the day. As you can well imagine, I have quite a number of matters to attend to and will have to identify the bodies upon my return. I would be grateful if you could stay on a little later than usual to assist me in preparing some notes."

"Of course," was all she found to reply.

She put the phone down and found her legs were trembling. Her hands also trembled as she attempted to dial down to the receptionist and ask that the staff be requested to meet her in the board room in fifteen minutes.

Oh my God, she said to herself. *The poor man must be devastated. How am I going to put this to the staff?*

Her last thought before leaving her office to go to the board room was, *what on earth could have made her do such a thing?*

THE DAUGHTER'S TALE

I n a certain fashion, they all learned of the tragic news in different ways.Even though it should never have happened in such a way; it is just one of life's injustices that news travels fast, and often those nearest and dearest do not get to hear of impending news, good or bad, prior to the media.

She had just arrived at her desk in the office that sunny morning prior to picking up the paper. She was in a good mood, having spent a great weekend with friends, some of whom were also colleagues at the fashion magazine where she was presently doing a six-month project for college.

Life seemed to be going pretty well right now; she and her father were now on fairly good terms, after quite a long split, all this having been caused by his remarrying so soon after divorcing from her mother.

Her mind went back to this period in time. She had not thought it possible to be as angry with anyone as she had been with him when he had told her of his decision. This had happened just after her first year away in the States; she had been more than happy that she was away from all the mess. Her brother had told her how bad things had been, and she felt for her mother. However, she had not felt so sad for her as the deep resentment she felt against her father. How on earth could he have done such a thing? He had married someone almost her age (well, only five years older). It was disgusting, she had thought at the time, and had for a time hated her father for pushing his real family aside. There had always been a little wall of conspiracy between them, something her mother knew but did not exactly approve of.

"You spoil her too much," she had often heard in the house. These words came from her mother's mouth and were meant for her father. He had always replied the same thing, words that she would never forget:

"I know that I spoil her, but I love her so and am so proud of her."

"So am I," her mother used to say. "But I worry that she will grow up spoiled and capricious."

She had grown up, and yes, perhaps her mother had been correct. She had been spoiled and could be capricious when not getting her own way, something she very much liked; she was growing to learn, albeit the hard way, that this was not always possible.

Finally, her father had accepted her wishes to study overseas, and she knew that his approval was due to her mother's subtle handling of the situation. She missed her mother a lot but spoke to her regularly, twice a week, on the phone. She seemed really happy these past months, and she had begun to wonder if she had met someone else. *That would be great for her*, she thought, *and just what she needs.* She had even asked her mother, who had just laughed at the suggestion and told her not to be silly. She had been so convinced that something was going on that she had phoned her brother and asked him if he knew anything.

"No Sis," he had replied. "Maybe you're right, but I don't know anything, and Mum has not mentioned anybody in particular."

She had to be content with that, at least for the time being. Mum seemed to have changed; she could not explain what she meant, it was just that her voice seemed different, as if there was electricity in the air. "It's all in your imagination," her brother had told her mockingly, and maybe it is, she told herself.

She had changed since her last visit to Grandma's for her seventy-eighth birthday. *Perhaps she had met someone up there*, she thought. *Well, time will tell.*

Her thoughts went to Grandma. It was, in a way, Grandma who had given her the love of fashion. Many years ago, when she had been little, she had often stayed overnight with her, and although she could be quite strict, just like Mummy, Grandma adored her little granddaughter, who was the image of her father, with his dark eyes and black hair. She wore her hair tied back, and Grandma or her mother would see that she had a different coloured ribbon every day. She had loved when Granny brushed her long hair over and over again, telling her how pretty she was. Her mother was not so prone to complimenting her, even in those days, but between Granny and her father, she did pretty well. When she was about six years of age, she heard the word "wealthy" for the first time. She did not know its meaning but knew that it meant something good. Things had begun to change. First they moved into a really big house, one in which she did not have to share a bedroom with her younger brother. He was still a baby as far as she was concerned, and her mother always seemed to be fussing over him and giving him lots of cuddles, far more she ever did with her. However, she had accepted this as part of life, after all, she had Daddy and Granny to fuss over her.

At primary school, she had done very well and was always in the top three. The teachers always had a kind word to say about her, and she found herself often running home with yet another gold or silver star in her school notebook. Life had been so easy then, and she never wanted it to change.

But life does change, she remembered. When she had been twelve, the family decided to move away from the North and to another country 3,000 miles away. Granny decided not to come with them, despite all of their efforts to make her change her mind. But as always, she had been adamant.

"Come and visit me during your school holidays, and in the summer you can stay for a long time," she had told her grandchildren. "I am too old now to be changing my lifestyle." And so it was; the four of them moved away, to a new country, a new school, a new home, and above all, a new language.

Changing schools at twelve is never easy, but changing countries is an entirely new way of life and quite a difficult task for a young girl. She remembered so well her first day at school, how she had hated it. She did not know anyone, and she missed her old chums more than ever. She had been sent to an international school, which she hated, and made up her mind, from day one, to make life a misery for everyone, including her teacher and her parents.

It was perhaps at that moment in time that her father took her under his wing. He had protected her, dried her tears, tucked her into bed at night, and told her that everything was going to be all right. She had to learn to adapt and make new friends, he said, and soon she would see that life was not so bad.

"You have to give things time," he had told her one evening when he had come to say good night. Normally her father was right, she thought, so perhaps it will not always be like this.

"You know I do not like to see you unhappy; you are my little girl, my little treasure," he had called her.

She could only hope so. He began buying her small gifts, coming home with little surprises; he always brought the whole family lots of presents when he returned from of his business trips. It was also about this time she began to realise that she could get anything she wanted from her father, he spoiled her so. She now had a chauffeur who drove both her and her brother to school, and she rather enjoyed arriving at the school gates in this fashion. The chauffeur then took her father into the city.

One year later, she had settled down, more or less. Granny had visited them in their new home. "It's rather large," she had told them at table one evening. However, they all loved their home now and all that went with it. Her father now had his own offices in town and was becoming a well-known businessman. This is what her mother had told her, and she was proud of this fact.

In the summer, they had packed their cases and set off for a month at Granny's. This had been so much fun, and although her father did not join them, other than for a long weekend, she, her brother, and sometimes Mummy enjoyed swimming in the lakes, picnicking in the forest, and visiting old friends.

Life was much simpler at Granny's. She loved to go and sit with her while she was making dresses in all sorts of colour and material. She was sometimes allowed to help choose the colour and thread to be used. Granny had even allowed her to cut some material, and under her watchful eye, she began to love this work. It was so exciting seeing a skirt or a dress made up from a pattern. Granny had a steady hand for cutting and told her that one day, with a lot of practice, she could be just as good. She loved the sound of the sewing machines in the workshop which was a maze of pins and needles, dresses hanging everywhere, and measuring tapes lying about, either around Granny's neck or draped over a chair.

Therefore, it was not surprising that a few years later she decided that she wanted to study fashion. She did not just wish to make dresses but also to design them. As her final school exams came round, she was desperate to apply for a college in the States. It had been a long road, getting her father to accept this, but she had finally been given the green light.

It had never entered her head that she might not be offered a place she so coveted. The first college, however, did turn her down; however, her second application was successful, and she had never felt as excited or happy as the day her approval came.

The move had been more emotional than she could have imagined possible. Now she had to stand on her own and work hard, she had been told by both her parents, if she wanted to make it.

"Things may get tough, but you have to continue and never give up if you want success," her mother had told her the evening prior to her departure. Her father was flying over with her, and she was glad about that. She was more apprehensive than she wished to appear, knowing that she was going to be so far away from her home and family.

Her father had insisted that she live on the campus the first year, thus giving her time to settle and make new friends. If all went well and she succeeded, then he would consider buying her an apartment near the college which she could share with a girlfriend. However, there was a long way to go before that would happen.

The first few months had been difficult, although she loved her classes and coped as well as she could. She worked hard, as she was determined to pass her first year with flying colours; it had also helped that her father ensured that she wanted for nothing.

It was then that the news had come, like a bolt in the dark. He had been over to visit, and they had been out for dinner. He had seemed a little nervous, she had thought, but could not work out why. He always had things in hand, but when he told her that he had something important to tell her, her heart missed a beat. She felt somehow that this news was not going to please her. He took her hand in his and looked directly in her eyes before pronouncing the words that would change her life.

"There is no easy way to tell you this," he had finally spoken. "Your mother and I are going to separate."

"Separate?" she had said, repeating his word. "What do you mean?"

"I have met someone else; your mother is aware of this, and now it is my duty to tell you and your brother."

"Who is she and where did you met her?" she asked accusingly, suddenly feeling an anger boiling within her. She did not recognise this person sitting opposite her, this man who was telling her that he had met someone else. He had also added that she was young and that he hoped they would both, with time, become friends.

He had not answered her, preferring to remain silent. He had known this would not be easy, but his daughter made it clear that she wished nothing to do with her, refusing even to name his new girlfriend. She had left the restaurant in a blind fury and could not bear to see her father again. She had called her mother straight after, who had confirmed what he had just told her.

"Why did you not tell me?" she had asked her mother.

"Well, it was up to your father to announce the news. I thought it better that he tell you face to face."

"Are you all right?" she had asked.

"Well, I have known better days, but his mind is made up, and you know your father, when he decides something, there is no going back."

She had to admit that she was right on that point.

The next few days had been ghastly. She had felt permanently sick and refused all calls from her father. She had spoken to her mother every day, also her brother, who appeared as shocked as she was. However, nothing had changed; her parents had separated and, a few months later, divorced.

They had all been shocked that her father had married so quickly after his divorce. She had refused to attend the wedding ceremony, and no pleading from her father would make her change her mind. The vulgarity of the entire sordid affair made her ill, even to think about it, and the idea of being present at his wedding was something she could not stomach. She knew that her brother had gone, more out of duty than anything else, but she did not feel any such commitment.

And so the relationship between daughter and father had become strained. She made no effort to make things easy for him. She eventually agreed to meet him upon one of his business trips; the atmosphere had been cold, and she had done nothing to appease this. He, on the other hand, had tried to win back her affection, if not her love. *He no longer deserved it,* she had thought to herself at the time; *let him wait.* On reflection, she thought that she may have been too hard on her father; her brother had reminded her that, after all, it was he who picked up all her bills and who had bought her a lovely flat in a rather upmarket area. She knew all this and was, in some strange way, grateful to him, but she never thanked him, making him feel as though it was his guilty conscience that made him pay for her every whim.

She finally relented, and if things were never the same between them, at least they patched up their differences, and she made an effort to be more the daughter he wanted her to be. Her mother had also helped; she had flown over several times and told her that life had to continue and carrying on the way she was doing, she would alienate him forever.

"Is this really what you want?" she had asked her daughter. "You know very well that if you push him too far, he will drop you completely out of his life. We have all had to accept that he has a new life; I've done so, why can't you?"

Her mother had, of course, been right. And so her relationship with her father became warmer, and she tried to make up for some of the awful things she had said to hurt him.

Accepting his new wife, however, was another matter; she could still not make herself ask how she was or if he was enjoying his new life. Then there had been more news; she was expecting a baby. Another bitter pill to swallow, but she did and went on with her life. Now things were going well, and she was feeling a lot more confident. She had passed her second year without any problem and was now working at this fashion magazine, doing her project to complete her third year. Life was taking shape again, and she realised how correct her mother's words had been. Also, her mother was very happy these past months. Her mother gave nothing away, and although she had plagued her brother, he told her that he knew nothing. He had always been very close to his mother and saw her regularly, so she was sure that if anyone would know something, it would be he.

"Mum will tell us when she is ready," he had told her last week on the phone. "Just be patient, and in time you will hear."

What on earth he had meant by that remark, she had no idea. Surely her mother would have told her if there was someone serious in her life. *Wouldn't that be great for her?* she thought, taking a mint out of her handbag and hearing one of her colleagues ask if she wanted a coffee. After replying that she would love one, she idly picked up the morning paper which she had bought on her way to the office. With all these thoughts in her mind, she had not had time as yet to glance at the headlines.

"Oh my God," she said as she read the glaring headlines: "Woman and baby die in suicide furnace."

She read on with interest, wondering who could possibly carry out such a terrible act. It appeared that the woman had set the baby alight before turning herself into a walking flame. It was too horrific for words. She jumped as her phone rang, her thoughts still with the contents of the newspaper lying in front of her.

She noticed that it was her father's mobile number.

"I have been trying to get you since yesterday," he said quietly.

"Oh, I was away for the weekend and left my mobile at home. What's up, Dad?"

"I have some very bad news to tell you, although you may have already seen it in this morning's paper."

She suddenly knew without doubt what he was going to tell her, and her heart skipped a beat.

"Don't tell me it's about the suicide," she said, her mouth drying up with fear at what he was going to say.

"It is, my dear," he replied in a whisper. "My wife committed this act of folly and took the baby with her in her plight."

She did not know what to say. The silence that hung in the air was crushing.

"Daddy!" she cried out in a voice that sounded as though she was six years old again. "Oh my God, why on earth would she do such a terrible thing?"

"It's my fault," he answered.

"How can it be your fault?" she asked. "She must have been crazy."

"No, it is entirely my fault, but we shall talk about this another time.

"I have to go now as I have many other calls to make. Take care sweetheart and I'll phone you again later on today"

She could not answer much as she struggled to say "I love you Dad"

She put down the phone, holding on to her desk for support. *What has happened?* she thought. *Why would she do this?*

The news would not be long in reaching her.

THE LOBBYIST, PART 3

He drove into the city car park that morning and proceeded to make his way to his offices on the second floor.

His secretary was already there, and he smelt the aroma of coffee being made; just what he needed, he thought. He saw that his paper was lying on his desk and a couple of bagels were already on a tray, awaiting the coffee.

He shouted good morning to her, but as he got no reply, he guessed that she was more than likely putting some perfume on in the restrooms or making some of her endless photocopies—copies that she was eternally making for either himself or his partner.

She was a real pearl, and they had been lucky to find her. A young lady in her midthirties, pleasantly attractive, but in a quiet and demure fashion; she was also devoted to the two partners and the company, and nothing was too much to ask of her. *Always the first in and the last out of the office*, he thought to himself. *I really must get around to having her salary reviewed.* He would get that matter done this week.

He idly picked up the newspaper lying on his desk and read the headlines.

"Young mother commits suicide along with her 8-month-old baby."

"Oh my God," he said out loud. "Why on earth do people do such things?" he remarked to his secretary, who had just entered the room with his morning coffee.

He quickly began to scan the news item.

"I haven't as yet read the paper," his secretary answered him, putting the tray on his desk. "What's happened anyway?"

"This suicide is so unbelievable," he said, continuing to read the paper.

"Oh that," she said. "Yes, I did see the newspapers headlines; it all sounds pretty awful to me. They seem to think that she is of Islamic faith," she went on. "They seem to like these horrific deaths."

"Yes, it might well be true what you are saying," her boss said, "but they are not all like that. I remember meeting one several years ago. I met him on a plane; we were sitting together, and as he got up to leave the plane, he gave me his business card and asked that I contact him.

"Strange really, but you know we became friends after a while. In fact, we are still continuing to do business with him; you know the casino project that we have been working on recently? Well, this friend was the brains behind that one, not to mention the money. All done through foundations, mind you; he does not like his name being mentioned, preferring to work behind a facade of companies, but one thing is certain, he is a good man and a good Muslim."

"I don't remember meeting him," the secretary continued.

"No, you were not here when we commenced the project. At that time, he was often in town and actually came to my wedding. You know, in a strange way, I got to like him, although it had not started out that way." He laughed as he remembered how they had become good friends.

His friend had remarried shortly after a rather hostile divorce which had almost ruined him financially. He had felt for him and tried to work on his project and get the adequate backing necessary for such a venture. His father had been a great help to him, and for once he had felt that was doing something for somebody without looking out for his own financial gains. He liked the feeling this gave him.

He remembered that when he and his wife had married last year, he had invited his friend to the wedding along with his new wife. He had found her to be rather plain and shy and could not help wondering what had made him divorce his first wife to marry this rather timid creature. She had appeared lost among the golf crowd that was his own and had said very little to anyone. He had noticed at the time that she did not drink any alcohol either. He had remarked at their wedding that she had been married under Islamic law, thus she had surely converted to Islam for his sake. He could not imagine his friend imposing any type of religion upon his family; he had known for a fact that in his first marriage, neither his wife nor his children had been brought up into the Muslim faith, but perhaps, he thought, this was one of the conditions in marrying this young girl, that she convert. Well, that was their problem and not his, he thought to himself in the office that morning.

He knew that there had been a baby girl the previous year, so maybe she had been pregnant at the wedding, thus making her overly shy and perhaps a little bit distant. His friend had actually never told him where he had met her; he knew that it was on one of his many business travels, but somehow he could never quite bring himself to ask how and why. To anyone else he would have asked, no joked, about the matter, but not his friend. Perhaps out of loyalty or out of trust, he could not answer this question even to himself. However, things were as they now stood, and although he had no empathy towards the young girl, he refrained from making any comment on the matter.

Lost in his thoughts, he turned around in his chair as his phone rang. He was happy to see from the number that it was his father calling. He and his father had become very close over the past couple of years. He knew that this was partially due to the fact that he married and settled down, but he also felt that his father was proud of his son, knowing that he was now involved in some humanitarian issues, something which had not always been his case. Only last week, his wife had said that she was pregnant with their first child; they had not already announced this to his parents, but he knew that they would be overjoyed at the news. Yes, life was pretty good right now.

His father, after asking him how he and his wife were, went on to tell him that the ongoing project regarding the building of a new airstrip was now seriously being discussed amongst the powers that be.

"It's looking pretty good, son," his father told him. "I would not be surprised if we can get this baby to bed before the end of the next sitting. However, let's not jump the gun. There are still a few powerful voters to give their benediction on this one, but honestly I think we may be able to overcome this. As usual, there are always the environmentalists to deal with; to say the least, they are not at all in favour of polluting the area with numerous flights taking off and landing, but if we can come to some arrangement and provide some compensation to their cause, a large donation, plus a few titbits here and there, I think we can nail it."

"That's great news," his son replied. "You have been such a great help on this one, and I know that we are going to pull it off; the celebration dinner is on me."

"Well, let's wait and see; another few weeks and we should know a little more on how the voting is going to proceed, but in the meantime, I thought you would like to be kept aware of the situation."

"I certainly do, and I shall give our friend a call to put him in the picture also. I know that he is going to be very pleased with the news."

Putting down his phone, he thought how much this news would mean to his dear friend. On his last trip to Europe, he had found him to be tired and restless, almost as though he had something on his mind that was plaguing him. He had never said as much, but he had sensed at their last dinner meeting that something was not quite right. He had not wished to pry and decided to leave well enough alone; *I shall speak to him again on my next trip and see if I can get him to open up a little,* he thought.

The only thing that he had learned was that his friend had met up rather unexpectedly with his ex-wife on some trip or other. He could not remember the details, but it appeared that they had met by chance on a plane. He had said nothing else, but he did wonder if there was more to this matter than a chance meeting. His friend had recently become a father again for the third time, and he had seemed to be happy about this event. So why would a chance meeting with his ex bring him so much pain? Or was it pain?

He remembered tenderly how he had met his wife in the French bistro, their first date, their engagement followed by a society wedding. Now she was going to have a baby, and the thought filled him with joy; yes, life could not be better.

He made up his mind to give his friend a call later on; he would await the morning mail and catch up on some letters prior to phoning. He went into his briefcase when his mobile rang. From the number, he recognised immediately that it was his European friend; he was glad, this would give him the chance to relate the news his father had just given to him.

"Hi," he said. "My father and I were just talking about you; your call could not come at a better time. I have some good news to give you."

There was a silence at the end of the line, and he could barely make out the words that were being said.

"Why were you talking about me?" the voice asked. "Have you read the papers this morning?"

"Not really," the lobbyist said. "Just the headlines about a young woman and her baby who died at the airport; what a tragedy! Did you hear about it?"

"Yes," his friend replied. "Actually, that is the reason for my call this morning."

The lobbyist said nothing, but he sensed that there was some bad news on the way.

"That was my wife and daughter" was all he could say.

The lobbyist found that for once in his life, he was unable to answer and had no words to comfort his friend.

The following silence was penetrating, as he finally found the words.

"Oh my God, I am so sorry; what on earth could have possessed her to do such a terrible thing?"

"I really do not know, at least for the time being," his friend answered. "I just wanted to let you know as soon as possible, to tell you personally; that is important for me."

"Can I do anything for you, be of any assistance to you?"

Even to the lobbyist, his words felt shallow, but he felt the need to say something; he would have done anything to help his friend.

"No, thank you, but perhaps next week."

"Sure, anytime, give me a call and let me know. Do you wish me to fly over?"

"No thanks, not for the time being, perhaps later on. I shall be in touch shortly," his friend said, after which they said their good-byes.

The lobbyist stood dumbfounded, staring at both the phone and the newspaper still on his desk.

His heart ached for his friend; why had she done such an awful thing? Surely time would tell. He called through to his secretary and asked for another coffee.

"And please make it very strong," he added. "Also hold all my calls for the rest of the morning."

His secretary popped her head through the doorway and asked him if everything was all right.

"Not really," he answered her, "but I shall let you know this afternoon when I have some more details. My dear friend has a problem, and I just do not know how I can help him. Perhaps I shall have to leave for Europe within the next few days; please have a look at the flights over the next few days. It will only be for a few days, and then I shall be returning back home."

"Fine," she answered, closing the door every so quietly. Something had upset him, and she had no idea what it could be. She had never seen him look so pale and upset. No doubt he would tell her what was bothering him later on this afternoon; she only hoped it was nothing too serious.

THE INQUEST VERDICT

The inquest was held on a springlike day several weeks later, towards the end of June. As he walked towards the courtroom, he noticed that the roses were beginning to bloom.

How strange, he thought, *that after all this time and all these years, I can now see their pastel colours and take in their beautiful scent.* The delicate lemon and pale Indian roses were all new to him; he, who had ordered many bouquets of roses, was suddenly ashamed that he had never stopped to breathe in their beautiful, sensual scent. He knew well that normally he would never have observed such matters, but life had changed for him over these past two months; having to identify his wife and baby's bodies had been an ordeal that he felt he could never overcome and something he hoped never to have to go through again. It was as though he was being sentenced to a life sentence, one where he had done nothing to deserve such a punishment, but deep down he felt that the invisible jury had unanimously sentenced him to a life of guilt and suffering.

She had wanted him to suffer, to serve life, not perhaps in jail, but in another fashion. That had been her choice for him, and had it not been for the love and loyalty of his family, he would have fallen into the trap she had so cleverly laid. He would never understand why she had done this to him—he, who had fallen in love with her freshness and innocence, had never completely understood how she had become twisted and fanatical. No, he had never wished this and had done all in his power to avoid her becoming too involved with religion. He had made his fatal mistake in not being there for her. She had gone her own way, decided her own fate, hoping to drag him also in her downward spiral. This would have been her triumph, her last cherished wish that he suffered on this earth for the rest of his life.

However, she had been wrong; the love he had found within his first family had assisted him in this horrific passage in time, one in which he hoped and prayed no other man would have ever to go through. His children had been wonderful, and as for his first wife, she had said little, but her presence was enough for him to get up every day and begin to put his life straight once again.

He had been so ashamed—he, who had never given a moment's notice as to what others thought, had begun recently to feel that all eyes were now upon him, wondering what terrible thing he had done, to make a young girl take her life in such a manner.

He had avoided the office for the first few weeks, preferring to deal with his PA and his PR, either speaking to them on the phone or having them come up to the villa. He did not wish to show his face but knew eventually that he would have to and that his staff would expect that of him; he owed them this, and so with time, he had started driving to the office and spending at least half a day there. It had been good for him, and people had been more than sympathetic.

The first morning he made his way back to the office, he had looked in the mirror and barely recognised himself.

He had aged five years in a few weeks; his eyes were those of a man who had seen death but who had survived. He felt an emptiness he could not explain, and his hands trembled now, something he knew was temporary, but the dice had been thrown, and now it was his turn to change his destiny. He knew that it would be difficult, but he was determined that he would be capable.

Now as he sat down in the coroner's office, he heard them read out that it had been a clear-cut act of suicide; this had come after listening to his wife's doctor, who had explained that she had been suffering from severe depression since the birth of the baby. *Depression?* he had thought to himself; he had not even noticed that she had been down, never mind severely depressed. His thoughts had been elsewhere, and certainly not with his wife and new baby. *He should have noticed the cry for help*, he thought, but her cries had gone unheeded, and now it was too late.

It was all over; fifteen minutes within a courtroom and two people's lives were now a statistic, a closed book, and the contents therein, ready for classification.

He had planned a memorial service for his wife and baby daughter. This could not be held until the coroner and the court had delivered their verdict. They had both been buried as quickly as was possible, following the Muslim ritual which he knew would have been her last wish and something he could not deny her.

His friend the lobbyist had been a tower of strength during this period, as had various members of his staff, in particular his PR and PA. They had asked no questions and had said very little, something for which he was eternally grateful. No pointing fingers, no accusations, just a few kind words, and he knew that these people could be trusted, no matter what.

He had blamed himself so much at the beginning. He, who had left his family for his faith and religious principles, only to return to them in order to find the love and comfort he so desperately needed. He had realised, perhaps too late, that they possessed everything he had been searching for in life—it had been there in front of him all these years.

Had his faith let him down? Or had he let his faith down? He had no answer to these questions and wondered sometimes if he ever would.

His wife and baby were now at peace; this was a fact that he had to live with on a daily basis. He had to move on, put the past behind him, and find the peace in this life that she had found in the next.

Time alone would tell him if he had the capacity.

EPILOGUE

As he looked around, he saw that they had all come to the memorial service. He had hoped that they would, but had not been sure.

He noticed his assistant and her husband, his ex-wife, his PR manager and his family, and his friend the lobbyist and his wife, who had flown in yesterday for the service.

Both his children were there. His daughter had flown in last week from the States, and his son also had come to be with him in his time of need. He had not spoken in great detail about the incident, and they had not asked too many questions. They had both been shocked at the news and could not imagine that she had taken the little one with her. They had grown to be very fond of her, and in a strange way, he was comforted by the fact that the baby's death had saddened them so much.

He knew that their mother had spent a great deal of time with them and that she had smoothed over the event as much as possible.

His time would come later; they would need answers, that he knew, and in time they would receive all that he had to give them. There would be time for all that later.

He stood inside the mosque with his head bowed, praying silently. He felt a great sadness, that in her flight from this life, she had chosen to take the baby too. And yet, in the strangest of ways, he understood why his wife had committed this appalling act. In a certain way, it was to prove to him that she was going to a place where he may never go, and if that was the case, then, she had won.

His ex-wife walked over, stood beside him, and took his hand in hers, clasping it tightly within her own.

She knew that in time, things would get better. The papers would cease to talk about the entire unfortunate incident, and life would eventually, one day, get back to something resembling normality. The family had been through so much over the past month, and although it was far too early to plan anything, she knew that she would win her husband back and that one day in the not-too-distant future, he would return home to her and his family. But for now, he needed to grieve, but she would ensure that she was there for him and that he would not be alone in his despair.

As the imam began his speech, she like the others bowed her head in prayer.

Tomorrow is another day, someone had once said, and for her it could not come quick enough; she closed her eyes.

Yes, she repeated, "tomorrow is another day," recalling the famous words of Scarlett O'Hara.

Quite appropriate, she thought, smiling sadly, but without any tears.

Life will go on, she told herself, *and we shall all survive this*. She stopped thinking as she bowed her head, having heard the imam start to chant.